This delightful collection of stories portrays the antics of "small people" who want to act "big," so as to portray themselves bigger than they really are. The main players include Blake (the Snake), Jeff (the Nose), Billy (the Mackster), Sy (Slo-Mo), and Wesley (Tex). Some of the stories are serious, and many are humorous. *Blake "the Snake" Sloan and Friends* is a great reading activity targeted to teens but can be enjoyed by almost all ages.

Blake "The Snake" Sloan and Friends...

Making it Through Middle School!

Delbert "Delby" Pape

iUniverse LLC
Bloomington

**BLAKE "THE SNAKE" SLOAN AND FRIENDS...
MAKING IT THROUGH MIDDLE SCHOOL!**

iUniverse books may be ordered through booksellers or by contacting:

iUniverse
1663 Liberty Drive
Bloomington, IN 47403
www.iuniverse.com
1-800-Authors (1-800-288-4677)

Because of the dynamic nature of the Internet, any web addresses or links contained in this book may have changed since publication and may no longer be valid. The views expressed in this work are solely those of the author and do not necessarily reflect the views of the publisher, and the publisher hereby disclaims any responsibility for them.

Any people depicted in stock imagery provided by Thinkstock are models, and such images are being used for illustrative purposes only.

Certain stock imagery © Thinkstock.

ISBN: 978-1-4759-9894-8 (sc)
ISBN: 978-1-4759-9893-1 (hc)
ISBN: 978-1-4759-9892-4 (e)

Library of Congress Control Number: 2013912541

Printed in the United States of America.

iUniverse rev. date: 7/22/2013

The itsy bitsy spider went up the water spout.
Down came the water and washed the spider out.
I picked the spider up and tried to put it in Bobbi Sue's snout.
I got in trouble from my teacher, Ms. Sherridon, without a doubt!

To my elementary school buddies.
I don't know where they all are now, but I have
fond memories of them to this day.

Rusty—Are you still as fast as you were in the fourth and fifth grade at Travis Elementary School in San Angelo, Texas? I never could beat you in the fifty-yard dash—nobody ever did—but I came close a time or two! Do you remember Ms. Newhouse and Principal Lark? Did you ever grow over five feet tall?

Larry—We had a fight once after school, and when Principal Lark heard about it, he and Coach Little got us out of class the next day. They put boxing gloves on us and had us go after each other. The one not *getting it on* got wacked on the behind with a spat board. This went on until finally our hands were drooped from holding the boxing gloves up. We were extremely tired, but not so much from hitting each other with the gloves. Wow, my butt hurt for a long time afterward. That incident made us come to a different point of thinking, and we became friends after that. I'm glad we did!

Nancy—Was there ever a day you weren't pretty? Wow, what a gal!

Bev—Sorry we lost you in the seventh grade to a car accident. I have fond memories of the *Travis Raiders* boys playing on the playground.

Billy—A fun guy but moved to California in the sixth grade. Where are you now?

Johnny—Had lots of good times playing baseball at the local park with you and the neighborhood kids.

Mark—Side-street football in front of your house was the best. We got in a lot of trouble from your dad when we knocked the *not ready to pick* apricots off his tree.

Wanda—As pretty as Nancy, and some said you liked me. I should have followed up on that.

Emory—Are you still bullying others? I hope not.

Jerry—You were always so smart. I bet you're a millionaire by now.

Bob—You were the biggest and baddest cowboy I ever knew. You were our hero when you moved in from Oklahoma and put Emory in his place. Thanks from all of us.

Table of Contents

Introduction

Name: Blake Sloan

Nickname: "The Snake"

School Name: Grape Field Middle School

School Mascot: Surfer Joe

Best Friends:
- Jeff McCoy (Nickname: "The Nose")
- Billy Mack (Nickname: "The Mackster")
- Sy Wilcox (Nickname: "Slo-Mo")
- Wesley Strait (Nickname: "Tex")

Favorite Food: PPJ sandwiches

Favorite Movie: *Dumb and Dumber*

Favorite Dessert: Ice cream dripping with chocolate syrup and lots of nuts

Favorite Saying: "You scream, I scream, we all scream for ice cream!"

Vocabulary Exercise For Each Selection

Choose <u>three</u> words that you would like to better understand the meaning.

Write a definition for each word.

Use each word in a sentence you create.

Draw a picture of the image you get in your mind for each word.

First Day of School

What? The text books are gone! What will we do?

Hello. My name is Blake Sloan. My friends call me Blake the Snake. My dad is a grape farm manager. We just moved from Eugene, Oregon, and I'm a little concerned about my first day of school in this new place and meeting and making new friends. Well, off to school I go!

"Good morning, class. I am Ms. Rothchild, and I will be your fourth-grade learning facilitator this year. I welcome you all to Grape Grove Elementary School, the newest elementary school in the Napa Valley area of California. I have good news. This school is the most technologically advanced to date. Look around the room, and you will see that there are *no* books. All of the information from textbooks will be found online and accessed from your individual student computer.

"As you can see, each student desk cubicle area has a computer. The computer is located directly in front of you in the locked compartment. Each desk has an electric pencil sharpener and is mounted just to the right side of your desk. On the back left side of your desk, you will notice a small, mounted container that will be used for trash depositing. In front of that are two mounted, narrow containers that you will use to deposit completed assignments that are not computer related, as directed by yours truly ... me.

"Further, hard-copy notes and letters will no longer be sent home to parents, as these will come directly to you through your e-mail, and you will be responsible to then forward them to your parents. If you will look directly behind and at the rear of the classroom, you will notice two very wide doors. Once these doors are opened, you will see a nicely furnished lounge. As each period ends, you will have a ten-minute break and access to this area for your enjoyment and relaxation.

"This area is equipped with a surround-sound system that is connected to a 105-inch flat-screen television and entertainment center. The latest video games are available, as are light snack foods. This is the area where we will, beginning tomorrow, start our morning activities and obtain announcements from the main office. I'll give you more information later, but for now I'd like us all to introduce ourselves to each other. Let's begin with Georgia."

"Good morning, Ms. Rothchild. My name is Georgia Jean Hathaway. I was born and still live here in Napa. My daddy came from a banking background, and we live in the old Willford mansion on Cotton Wood Drive just south of here. As I look out the window, I can see the top of our home in the distance. It's the one on the top of the hillside. That's all I have to say."

"I'm Sy Wilcox, but my friends call me Slo-Mo. You can call me almost anything, but please don't call me too late to eat. I love to eat. My parents started the Hensley Steakhouse back in 1973. We now operate three others as well. We enjoy skiing for family fun. We go skiing every December at Cloud Croft, New Mexico, for our winter vacation. I'm especially looking forward to this year's vacation so I can get better at my skiing skills, as I get to go on the big-hill ski jump this time."

"Hello, my name is Pricilla Kay Keaton. My grandmother is Mary Kay, and she does cosmetics to help pretty girls look prettier. My parents own and operate the distribution center for my grandmother's cosmetics. I won my first beauty contest pageant this past summer and expect to win many more."

"Hi! I'm Billy Mack, the Mackster, and I like to run and play football. I'm already the quarterback for the Pee Wee Giants. Coach Watkins says our team is going to go undefeated this year as long as I'm the quarterback. See ya at the game."

"Yo. What's up! I'm Trevor Walker, and I play football with the Mackster. My dad is the coach of the Pee Wee Giants, and I'm the best football receiver there is. Coach told me we're going to go undefeated this year as long as I'm the receiver. Coach says I'm the best receiver ever, and the Mackster told me that too, and he's the best quarterback ever. So, come out and watch us this next week. We'll be there ... hope to see you there too!"

"My name is Angelina Faye Cash. My grandparents were

3

famous country singers. My daddy is their son, and he and my mom operate the royalties from some of their enterprises. I hope to be a singer someday, as I'm taking voice lessons and can already play the piano and violin. When I get to middle school, I'll be in the band. I can hardly wait for that to happen."

"Aaron Cartwright. My parents operate the Drury Inn Suites here in Napa. I like to spend some of my Saturdays there with my dad. I get free food at breakfast and dinner. I also like to play hide and seek there with my older sister. Dad allows us to play if we don't get too disruptive. Also, I would like to say I really like this new school. I like the way the lights automatically come on when I walk into the rooms and restrooms. That's really cool!"

"Amy Colgate here. My dad runs the plant that makes everybody have a beautiful and healthy smile. I live across the street from Georgia Jean. Hello again, Georgia. I'm glad we're in the same class together. This year is going to be the best! This weekend, our family will see some good ole 49er football. If Trevor and Billy realize that there's no I in team, then maybe I'll be able to see them play college ball someday. So when you do, I'll be there to watch you guys play."

"Beau Beauregard is my name, and riding my go-cart is my game. I'm a descendent of a famous general of the great Confederate States. My dad is chief executive officer (CEO) of Beauregard Enterprises, which specializes in government contracts in the greater Napa area. My most favorite thing to do is to ride my go-cart with my neighborhood buds. There's a track behind my house, and about five of my friends are usually there riding until dark or dinnertime. We have a blast!"

"Hi. My name is Nancy Intwissle. I am a foreign exchange student. I come from a small farming community in Norway. I am staying in the United States with my grandparents, and then

I will return to Momma and Poppa at the end of this semester. I'll be home just in time for Christmas, and I will get to see my school friends and tell them about my stay in this country. I hope to get acquainted with all of you. Thank you."

"Aye, what's up, Doc? My name is Jeff McCoy. Everyone around here calls me the Nose. I come from a long line of comedians. Always remember that the Nose knows. The Nose sees all, it knows all, and the Nose is all knowing. Got the picture? I had an uncle that used to say, 'I don't get no respect.' He said his wife is so ugly that once he parked his car and helped his wife get out. When she got out, a man walking by looked at her and then turned to him and said, 'I'm sorry.' My uncle then turned to him and said, 'Yeah, but she sure can cook.'

"And I have a cousin from my mom's side that makes a lot of money doing a show that has a lot to do about nothing. He's the real tall one and always has trouble walking and stumbles most of the time. And I have—"

Ms. Rothchild interrupted, saying, "Thanks, Jeff, that will be enough. Next student please ... wait. I appreciate all of the introductions. We have three other students that will be here starting on Wednesday, as soon as their summer cruise completes. We will be introduced to them upon their return. Now, we have one last student to hear from."

"Hello. My name is Blake Sloan ..."

Some Things to Think About

1. Would you like to go to this school?

2. What things do you do over the winter holiday?

3. Do you think this school would have different rules than other schools?

4. What things do you do with your family during the summer?

5. Which student or students would you like to hang around with the most?

6. Do you think the ten-minute break time should be longer?

7. What would you do during the break time?

8. Do you know where your parents work and what jobs they do?

9. What job do you want to do when you get older?

All aboard the Great RV Tour

A colorful blossom, a red flower, a
sweet-smelling beauty ... that's my Rose!

Hello again. It's me, Blake. It's been a year, and I'm a fifth-grader now. About two months ago, my dad bought an RV. He wanted our family to be close together and have some good times roaming around the world in it. He thought this would do the trick. He promised that he would let me have some friends over to spend the night in it too. That night finally arrived.

After school, my buds came over. We were excited! Jeff

arrived first. He has a really long nose, and I always tease him that his nose arrives three minutes earlier than the rest of him. That, of course, is an exaggeration, but it makes the point, and besides, he's a good-natured person and laughs right along with me. That must be why he's one of my best friends.

Shortly after Jeff arrived, Billy Mack strolled up. The Mackster was really enthused about this adventure. He had never been inside a real RV before. That's what I like about the Mackster; everything he sees is viewed as though it's completely new to him. This makes me get excited about things too, even though I may have seen them before. He helps me see a different view of things, which gives me a greater appreciation of that which I observe.

Finally, Sy arrived in his slow-moving way. We call him Slo-Mo because he moves so slowly. I slithered ahead and then motioned for them to follow me. Slo-Mo was last as usual.
I brought out the walkie-talkies and issued one to each of us. I assigned places to sleep, as we all decided we would sleep in the bunk section of the RV. Dad said we couldn't do any cooking, so Mom made us sacks of goodies, one for each of us.

We stayed up talking about things that happened at school the past week. Jeff the Nose said that Ross and Lacey were going steady. I asked him how he knew that. He laughed and said he had a nose for things like that. Then Slo-Mo reported he saw the principal kiss his teacher. We all reminded him that they *are* married. The Mackster looked at Sy and said, "You really are slow, aren't you!" They turned to me and asked if I had any news.

At first I couldn't think of anything really exciting that happened. But then I remembered we got a new student in our class, and her name is Rose. As I said this, all three of them looked at me and began asking all kinds of questions.

"I've heard about her!" the Nose exclaimed.

"I hear that she's a looker," added the Mackster.

"I can verify that she is indeed," I said.

"What's her name again?" asked Slo-Mo.

I told them that she came from Hawaii. I related that she has really nice, shiny, dark hair and shiny, dark eyes to match.

"Man, you're lucky that you have such a looker in your class," said the Mackster.

"Not only is she in my class, but she lives just three blocks from here," I said.

"No way," said the Nose.

"Oh, yeah ...way," I said.

About that time, Mom opened the back door, leaned out, and said for us to get ready for lights out. She turned off the back porch floodlight and told us good night. Dad added that he wanted our lights out in the RV within thirty minutes.

"Yes, sir," we all chimed back.

At eleven, Dad stuck his head into the RV and reminded us that it was time for lights out. We crawled into our places, and after the lights went out, we said good night to my dad.

Well, we continued our conversation for about thirty minutes longer, and it all centered around Rose. Then Slo-Mo got a brilliant idea. "Let's sneak over to her house," he said.

"No!" We all said at once.

"Come on. Let's do it," Slo-Mo came back with.

After a few more back and forths, we got out of bed, got out of our PJs, and put back on our clothes. As we eased out of the RV very quietly, I asked if everyone had their walkie-talkies, and Slo-Mo slithered back into the RV to obtain his.

About a half a block down the street, I gathered us together. I reminded them to keep their talkies on low volume and keep them close to their ears when talking over them.

We went a few more blocks, and I pointed to Rose's house.

"That's the one ... I think," I said as we edged a little closer.

We hunkered down between some bushes that were across the street from her house. Some lights were still on, and we could see movement inside. We were intent on our observing when we heard footsteps coming in our direction that couldn't have been more than twenty feet from us. Our heads turned toward one another, and we all put our forefinger to our lips so as to remind each other not to say a word. The footsteps stopped about ten feet away. It was my mom and my dad. They talked for a short while and then went on by and then across and down the street.

"That was a close one," I said after they were out of sight. "I guess they were out for a late stroll," I told my buds. We huddled and decided to meet in the alley in the back of Rose's house. This we did, with each of us leaving fifteen seconds apart. One by one, we gathered again at the designated place, and Slo-Mo was last to arrive.

"Guys, we have a problem," I stated.

The concern was that the fence was too high for us to see over. Heads together, we planned to scale the fence. I had to explain to Slo-Mo that to scale the fence meant that we had to climb over it. Well we did—climb over the fence, that is. The backyard was bushy and had three tall trees in it. I must admit it was a little scary looking. I turned my flashlight on and then quickly back off. I did that so we could orient ourselves to our surroundings. Each of us took a position and waited.

A short while later, I heard coming from my talkie, "This is the Nose ... I see movement." We all relayed back through the talkies and confirmed the same. The Mackster then reported that someone was approaching the back sliding door.

"It's Rose," I said.

Rose slid open the back door and said, "Go on, Lady, do your thing." Then a large, black and white spotted, barking dog came rushing out.

Four boys got a lesson and experienced their first heart attack that night. But no time for that as we scrambled around the yard, trying frantically to find the back fence. I heard the Nose say he was wrapped up and being eaten by a snake. I flashed my light in his direction and saw that he was tangled up in a garden hose, "Not a snake," I firmly stated. I continued toward the fence and was about halfway over it when I saw my three friends open the back gate, run through it, and into the alley. I felt like an idiot straddled across the fence.

A man came running out as I dropped my flashlight and bounded down the backside of the fence and onto the hard alley ground. It was easy to see which way the others had run, as I just followed the dust to the street. After that, I followed the smell of ... well ... you know, the burning of shoe rubber on asphalt. It didn't take me long to catch up with them.

Well, we made it back to the RV safe but not too sound. I had to listen to them whine about how I almost got them killed. I reminded them that it was Slo-Mo's big idea to go over there and *not* mine. Then the Nose started in on his nearly being eaten. "Yeah, by a garden hose," I reminded him. "Would you guys like some cheese with your whining?" I asked. That got us to laughing, and finally we nodded and then dosed off to sleep.

The next morning at breakfast, my mom and dad asked us what was going on at about midnight in the RV last night. We looked at each other and said, "What do you mean?" They explained that they heard us talking up a storm. "Oh, well," I said, "We thought we heard something outside".

"It must have been a bear," the Mackster blurted.

"Actually, I think it was a raccoon," I said, quickly recovering and motioning to him when my parents weren't looking.

"Oh, is that all?" my dad said. "I'm glad it wasn't a lion or a sea turtle. Well, anyway, I hope you guys had a fun time."

At school on Monday, Rose came up to me, handed me something, and said, "I think this belongs to you." I looked at what she gave me, and it was a flashlight that had my name engraved on the side of it. I looked up, and she was looking at me. Our eyes met, and we grinned … and then we laughed.

After school, I met up with my buds at the usual corner at the end of the school grounds. I told them that I talked to Rose. With clenched fists in my face, they immediately reminded me that I was not to say anything about our Friday night adventure. I backed away, and as they lowered their fists, I said, "Too late for that." I then showed them the flashlight that I had dropped while on our adventure. "She gave it to me this morning," I hurriedly stated. I showed them my name on the side of the flashlight, and then they understood.

Some Things to Think About

1. Do you have an RV, or do you know someone who does?

2. Have you ever spent the night in an RV or a tent in your backyard like these boys did?

3. What does your RV or tent look like?

4. Do you have a favorite experience to tell about? If so, tell or write about that favorite experience.

Those Big, White, Furry Things

Be on alert of older brothers or sisters
and their intended or unintended pranks!

We had many more adventures in the RV. On one occasion, at about one in the morning, I woke up from a noise coming from the underside of the RV. I staggered for my talkie, and after feeling around in the dark, I got a handle on it. With the talkie in one hand, I roused the Mackster with my other. I pressed the talkie talk button and relayed a message to Slo-Mo at the opposite end of the RV. Well, Slo-Mo didn't answer, so I tried the Nose and repeated the message:

"This here is the Snake. We got noise coming from underneath the RV. Get Slo-Mo up and quietly meet us in the middle of the RV by the refrigerator."

We all met at the designated spot but with more noise than was needed. After I got them quieted down to an acceptable level, we proceeded. I began to develop a plan of action when Slo-Mo opened the fridge.

"What the ... what are you doing? Close that door and get that light out," I demanded.

"I'm hungry ... and thirsty too," he said.

"Later, dude, but now we have a burglar to catch," I forcefully stated as I stared him down.

He slowly closed the fridge door, and we were back to our strategic planning. After my elaborate plan was presented and discussed, the Mackster said, "Why don't we just open the door and look outside?" We agreed, and then we argued among ourselves about who was going to be the one to open the door. After we heard "not me" four times, we decided to draw straws to see who would be the *lucky* one. The lucky one wasn't me, but it *was* the Nose.

We peaked out of the RV windows while the Nose cracked the door open and then stuck his nose, I mean head, out. He then quickly retracted himself and closed the door.

"I didn't see anything. Let's go back to bed," he whispered.

"That's because your nose was in the way," said the Mackster.

The Nose retorted with, "I'll have you know that the nose knows ... the nose knows where to go, look, and find ... the nose, it is all knowing."

While ignoring the Nose and his comments, the Mackster wedged himself between the Nose and the door. He put his hand on the doorknob and slowly turned it. With the door slightly open and I standing slightly to the left of him, I noticed that he rolled his eyes from side to side several times. He was calm, but then his eyes grew wide, and he quickly lunged himself backward while closing the door. He then placed himself against the door and said, "They're out there!"

"What? What's out there?" we as a chorus inquired.

"They're out there! They're out there! They're *all* out there," he repeated as he slumped down in a seat at the table. After I locked the door, the rest of us took a seat while six eyes focused on the Mackster.

"Would you like something to eat? I would. Maybe that will take your mind off of your delusional imaginings," said Slo-Mo.

"No, really. I saw six or maybe seven white, furry things running all over Blake's backyard," the Mackster replied insistently.

I asked the Mackster how he could see in the dark and then asked, "Are you a cat?"

He responded in the negative but reminded me that the quarter moon did provide some residual light. He then insisted we further investigate. I interrogated him like a detective asks questions to a suspect, and I determined the following:

- There were six or maybe seven white, furry *things* whizzing around the yard—*my* backyard!

- These *things* were about a foot tall.
- They had eyes that glowed brightly.
- They didn't make a sound.
- And, according to the Mackster, they could propel themselves upward from time to time.

I then proceeded to ask the Mackster, "When was the last time you had a chat with your psychiatrist?"

This got a few chuckles from the others and helped reduce our growing fears of our situation. But then I remembered a conversation my older brother was having with himself a few weeks earlier. He was discussing a project for his FFA (Future Farmers of America) class. All seniors had to have a project. As he was discussing several topics, I asked him who he was talking to, knowing full well it was to himself. He turned and said that he was having a really intelligent conversation with a very smart guy.

"Well," I said, "when you're through talking to him, come talk to the smartest guy in the world, me!"

He rolled his eyes and said, "No, really, Blake, I need some ideas for my FFA project. Do you have any?"

"Maybe. Maybe I do and maybe I don't. Actually, I do. How about a worm farm?"

With a wrinkled up nose, Bengy said, "A worm farm? Come on! I thought you were presenting yourself as the smartest person in the known world. Maybe your small, unknown *jungle* is more like it."

"Okay, let's stop the jostling," I said. "Here's one for you. I was seriously considering this one for *my* senior year, but since that's several years away, I'll stoop and save my brother from humiliation and share this with one of the underprivileged scoundrels of the world. What about rabbits? You can just raise them, or you can get the kind to show. There's money in it too, if you can place well in competition." His eyes glazed over, and he walked away while he rubbed his chin. I left him pondering and in a mused state, which was his natural state.

Are we really related? I asked myself. *Maybe the hospital staff got him switched by mistake, or maybe someone dropped him on his head when he was little and didn't say anything about it. Maybe he has an unknown disease that affects and stunts mental growth. Yeah, I'm sure that's it—the stunting of mental growth. That's got to be it. I'm sure.*

After relating that to my buds, I said, "That's got to be it— rabbits. Let's go check it out." And out the RV door we went.

Sure enough, there they were—rabbits running hither and thither and everywhere. Under the RV, around the RV, into the RV … what? Into the RV?

"Hey. Slo-Mo. No, never mind. Hey, Mackster, close the RV door quickly!" I stammered.

How many were there? Eight … ten … maybe a dozen or more. But one thing was for sure; there were a lot of them. And another thing was for sure; we were bound and determined to catch them. Come hail, sleet, rain, or snow, we were as determined to catch those rabbits as a mail deliverer is to deliver the mail.

Round and round we went, but an odd and puzzling thing was happening. We gathered in the middle of the yard for a meeting called by me.

"It's kind of dark out here," said Slo-Mo.

"Yeah, why don't we turn on the backyard floodlight so we can see. My eyes are playing tricks on me," said the Mackster.

"What do you mean?" I asked.

"I was chasing one of the critters, and just as I was reaching for him, he just disappeared," explained the Mackster. Nodding, we all agreed that had happened to us too.

The floodlight came on about that time, and we jumped from fright. We turned toward the light, and out stepped Bengy. He was on the bottom step of the porch, scratching his head with one hand and scratching his nether regions with the other. There he stood in his underwear looking like a poster child for rednecks.

I thought to myself, *Now if he only had on ...* In anticipation, my eyes scanned down to his feet, and sure enough there they were—dad's old combat boots on his feet, shoelaces untied naturally.

All eyes were focused on Bengy and his boots. Bengy's eyes followed our eyes to his feet, and then he looked up and stated, "I wasn't sure what I was going to find out here ... with the noise, the darkness, and all. I grabbed these boots 'cause I thought I might've had to kick some booty and become a neighborhood hero ... or something.

"Besides, what *is* this racket I hear going on?" he sleepily muttered. He seemed to be chewing on something too.

"Hey, Bengy, did you get some rabbits?" I piped up.

"Sure did. What's it to ya?"

"Are they magic rabbits?" I asked.

"No," he shot back. "They're over there in their pen I made for them. Old Man Jackson gave them to me for my FFA project. Pretty good idea I came up with, don't you think?"

"Hey, Boy Buzzard Brain," I said, "the rabbits are out running around in the yard, and we're playing tag with them."

"What? They got out? How? I know I shut the gate ... I think I did?"

"Boy Wonder, you never cease to amaze me. They're out, and we need your help catching them," I explained.

"And what's this about the rabbits disappearing on ya? My rabbits aren't magic. That's for magicians. But if they are of the magic kind, don't tell Old Man Jackson. Hey, I could make some real money on this project. Maybe a lifelong career too," Bengy dreamily stated.

"Bengy to earth! Bengy to earth! This is Blake, Blake the Snake. Come back down to this side of the galaxy please!" I said.

"I'm just joshing with ya. What do we have going on here, Blake ole boy?" Bengy asked.

"Rabbits," I explained. "We got rabbits *out*, and we need to get them *in*, but they're disappearing on us ... somehow."

"Blake, my man, show the Great One where they're vanishing from or to ... whatever," he stated.

Ignoring Bengy's haughtiness, I motioned them all over to the spot where mine had vanished. Bengy got down on his hands and knees and felt the grass. His head was about six inches from the ground. I told him how awkward he looked. We stood around laughing and cracking jokes at him. Bengy just continued on as if he didn't hear us. We kept up the wise cracking until Bengy stood up. We all quickly made apologies for our jokes, but Bengy said for us to get quiet, and we did.

Bengy stated that the mystery of the riddle had been revealed to him and he had the solution to the mystery of the vanishing rabbits. He said that the rabbits were real, and the magical vanishing of the rabbits was real too. He continued with a long dissertation on how we, the four of us, had disturbed the Underground Forces by our loud noises at extremely unnatural hours of the night. "This," he continued, "caused a shift in the polar caps, which sent unharmonious waves to our region. That, in and of itself," he theorized, "would not have completely done the trick. But add to that your obnoxious looks, and you have the total package for unleashing the Underground Forces upon the earth. The rabbits are disappearing, and you four are next!"

After I calmed down Slo-Mo, I asked Bengy, "What did you *really* find out?" He emphatically stated that the rabbits had gotten out of the cage and had dug holes in the yard, and those holes were where the rabbits were disappearing into, not into thin air. Bengy then stated that he was going to bed, and since it was the vibrations from our loud voices that caused the latch on the cage to come unhinged and let the rabbits loose, we had to round them back up and put them back in their cage.

"Good night," he said in a snickering way. "I'm going to bed."

This satisfied us, and we proceeded to round up the rabbits, cowboy style. We were able to get all eleven of them ... or were there supposed to be twelve? We secured the rabbits in a relatively quiet manner, so as not to disturb the Underground Forces, and then turned off the backyard floodlight. Too late for not disturbing the Underground Forces, as we noticed red flashing lights in front of our house as we walked toward the RV.

"Now what," inquired the Nose.

Some Things to Think About

1. Do you have an older brother or sister? If so, does the older brother or sister pester you, or is it you that does the pestering? Is he or she really smart sometimes and really not so smart other times?

2. If you think Bengy is cool, think of some ways in which he gives you this impression.

3. Have you ever petted a rabbit?

4. How many different colors of rabbits can you think of?

The Night My Mom Got Arrested ... Almost

What is black and white and goes real fast? A police car.

We all crowded close to the oversized driveway gate to get a glimpse of what the flashing red lights were about. I heard Slo-Mo say that we had disturbed the Underground Forces and that the Martians had landed—you know, the ones that control our sector of the universe. I told Slo-Mo to cut it out and stop joking, but I somewhat think he believed some of that stuff Bengy had said earlier.

We could hear voices coming from the car, like over some kind of a speaker. We saw the light from our front porch flash across the lawn. A police officer emerged from the police vehicle and started walking toward the front door, my front door. I looked in the direction of my buds and explained that the policewoman was probably lost and needed directions. They then asked me how I could know that. I explained that it was a lady cop and that a police*man* wouldn't have stopped and asked for directions. They all nodded their heads in the affirmative. Well, we were wrong.

We slowly and partially opened the side gate, just enough to slip through, and we then edged our way along the side of the house and snuggled among the lilac bushes. Now we were in a position to hear the conversation more clearly. What we were about to hear was something we weren't prepared for.

As it happened, my mom opened the front door. They introduced themselves to each other, and the lady cop said she was investigating a disturbance in the neighborhood. My mom related that she too had heard some noises and just got up to check them out when she noticed the police lights. My mom stated that she thought it might be coming from across the street.

"See, Officer Farley. Over there, the house with the lights on," my mom said.

About that time, we heard a voice from the direction of the house across the street say, "Here, kitty, kitty. Come on back in."

Officer Farley then said, "No, Mrs. Sloan. It was reported for *this* side of the street, but the address I have is one digit off from yours, and there isn't any other address close to it, except this one. I'll need to confer with dispatch. Knowing them, they may have gotten the street wrong too. I'll get this straightened out, and I'll be right back. Thanks for your patience."

Officer Farley walked back to her police car. She stayed there for a few moments as she talked to someone over the police radio. It was hard to make out what was being said, as the transmission was filled with static, and she was also too far away, but I thought I heard something about a burglary in progress. Officer Farley came back to the front porch and told my mom, "Well, Mrs. Sloan, I'm afraid they were no help and ...what was that noise?"

"I think your mom is about to be arrested," whispered Slo-Mo.

"Oh my gosh, you might be right," I said. "Shhh ... let's keep listening."

"What noise?" my mom asked Officer Farley.

"Over there. It came from those bushes," Officer Farley replied. "There it is again."

"I heard it that time," said Mom.

Before Officer Farley and my mom could get over to where we were, I reminded my buds to be quieter. They all insisted, in their softest voices, that they hadn't moved or made a sound. I ignored them and quickly reminded them to stay quiet, and then I said, "Here they come."

Officer Farley, my mom, God, and probably the burglar, were about to descend on us. We were going to be found out and taken to prison for disturbing the peace and letting the rabbits out of their cage because of our loud and excessive talking. Why couldn't we have just stayed in the RV and gone back to sleep? I don't know why, but I do know that we were in a lot of trouble, and my three buds, my mom, and I were about to spend some time in prison ... for a long time!

"Come out of there!" Officer Farley commanded. "Come out of there, I said," she repeated.

We didn't say a word. We were too scared to. We remained motionless, but I knew our rattling bones must have made noises that were louder than if we had been yelling and screaming. We glanced at each other as if to ask, "What are we going to do?" I didn't have the answer, and their eyes said the same. A scene flashed through my mind that showed Officer Farley jumping into the bushes and throwing us out one by one, handcuffed and stacked on top of each other, and then my mom was thrown on top of us all, handcuffed too. That thought was too much for me to handle, so finally I motioned for us to all step out. But wait a minute!

Something was rustling down close to me feet. I thought, *My feet aren't moving, and I hadn't seen anybody else move either.* Next thing I heard was my mom scream ... really loud! Now I *knew* my mom was going to jail.

"Well, would you look at that," said Officer Farley. "It's a rabbit. Are you the little feller that's been causing all the fuss? I guess I'm gonna have to cuff you and take you downtown."

Officer Farley looked at my mom and asked if she knew anything about the rabbit. She just shook her head and said that it *might* be one of the ones from her son's FFA project.

"Look, Officer Farley, how about I get my son out of bed and get him to put the rabbit back in its cage, real quietly like. What do you say?" said my mom.

"That sounds great!" said Officer Farley as she handed the rabbit to my mom.

"Thanks," my mom replied.

"No problem, Mrs. Sloan. I have a boy too," Officer Farley said as she turned to go to her police car.

As Officer Farley walked away, my mom stated, "We moms have to stick together."

Officer Farley did an about-face movement and said, "Don't push it, ma'am." She then winked, turned back around, and got into her police car.

I heard my mom repeat, "We moms have to stick together." Then she said, "What a dumb thing to say," as she went back into the house.

The Nose, the Mackster, Slo-Mo, and I didn't move until three minutes after the front porch light went out. Afterward, like unseen ghosts, we eased our way back through the gate and back into the RV.

A few minutes later, the back floodlight flashed on, and Mom lightly knocked on the RV door.

I asked her in my best sleeplike voice, "Is it time to get up?"

She cracked open the door and said, "No."

She said she wanted to make sure everything was all right. I assured her all was well. She said good night, and then we *all* said good night. As she closed the door, I caught a glimpse of a confused look on her face. She continued to the house, and then the floodlight went off. I heard Bengy call out to Mom to turn the light back on, as he hadn't gotten the door to the cage latched yet.

That night, four young boys promised one another never to let something like this happen again.

"Until the next time," said the Mackster jokingly.

"If something like this happens to us, we'll be in prison," replied the Nose.

"If what happens?" inquired Slo-Mo.

"Go to sleep!" I said.

Some Things to Think About

1. Wow, has anything like this ever happened to you?

2. How would you handle the situation?

3. Are these boys closer to one another because of this experience?

Graduating to the Sixth Grade

*What state is bigger than Texas? ... Alaska! ...
No! Not after you melt it down!*

"Sixth-graders rule!" we shouted as we entered school on the first day back. We had graduated from Grape Grove Elementary, and now here we were at Grape Field Middle School, and then eventually we'd go on to Green Grape High School to finish out. After a few days of school, I found out that sixth-graders don't really rule but are ruled by the eighth-graders. Man, I can't wait to be an eighth-grader!

After we got into the school year, my buds and I signed up for basketball, and we all made the team. At the beginning of the year, I got into band and played the trombone, or rather, played at the trombone. That's where and when I met Wesley Strait.

"You can call me Tex," he said when we introduced ourselves in band class.

Tex was a real cowboy and loved everything about Texas. His conversations revolved around Texas or something to do with cowboy-ing, ranching, roping, or riding horses. We got along real well right from the start. I played the trombone, and he played the drums. I was learning my instrument while Tex was already a pro.

Tex then asked me if I had ever heard about the elderly man that had real bad eyesight, and before he died he wanted to fulfill one of his dreams.

I asked Tex, "What dream was that?"

"To visit Texas, of course," he retorted. "Because he had always heard how everything was bigger in Texas. Well, the old gentleman was about to have his wish come true. He boarded the plane, and as he sat in his seat, he noticed something. He turned to a fellow sitting next to him and commented on how big the seats were. The fellow told him, '*Everything* is bigger in Texas.'

"Yes, sir," Tex continued, "they flew and landed in Dallas, Texas. They exited the plane, and the elderly man exclaimed how big the Texas sky was. The stewardess, overhearing, leaned toward him and reminded him, '*Everything* is bigger in Texas.'

"After leaving the airport, the elderly man found his way to a restaurant and quickly ordered a root beer, an A&W root beer, as recommended by the waiter of course. Well, the waiter returned with a mug of root beer and sat it down in front of the old man. The elderly man grabbed the mug and took a swig. Noticing how large the mug was, he excitedly told the waiter that it was a very large mug of root beer. As the waiter was walking away, he said to the old man, 'Yes, *everything* is bigger in Texas.'"

"Yeah, I get it. *Everything is bigger in Texas,*" I responded.

"Oh, but wait," Tex said. "After the old gentleman had finished the root beer, he then needed to go to the men's restroom and asked the waiter for directions. The waiter instructed him to 'Go through the double doors and take the second door to your left, and there they will be.'

"Sure enough, the elderly man went through the double doors, but after that, he became confused and took the third door on the left instead. This misdirection led him to the swimming pool area. He fell in the pool and frantically began splashing around and yelling at the top of his lungs, "Don't flush me down! Don't flush me down! Don't flush me down!"'"

Tex got me laughing on that one. I almost got detention from the band teacher.

Tex had a real knack for knowing what to say to people. Once we were in the cafeteria line, and three girls were up front giving the cafeteria workers a hard time about the food. Tex said sort of loudly, "Are there some mice in here? 'Cause I hear a lot of squeaking coming from right over there." Tex then pointed in the direction of the girls with his finger as if it were a gun.

The girls first looked at Tex and then tried to ignore him by turning back around and continuing their insults about the food. Tex then spoke up even louder. "I guess those door hinges need to be oiled, as they're still squeaking." He put the finishing touches on it when he turned to the rest of the students in line and declared, as loud as before and maybe a little louder, "I can't stand squeaky, disrespectful mice." This sent laughter through those standing around, and the girls went on their way without any further conversation.

We got our food and looked around the cafeteria to locate Slo-Mo, the Mackster, and the Nose. We spotted them, elbowed our way over to where they were sitting, and I related to them what had happened in the lunch line. Tex reiterated that he didn't like to see elderly folks disrespected. After looking around, Tex excused himself but said he'd be right back. We continued eating, and a minute or so later, I looked up and saw Tex talking with the girls from the lunch line. They were talking and laughing and having a good time from the looks of things.

Shortly thereafter, Tex came strolling back, sat down, and with his hand he waved a piece of paper under our noses. Surprised by this behavior, we asked what that was all about. He arrogantly stated that he had in his possession one of the girl's cell number. Disbelieving, we exclaimed that it was probably fake.

"Okay," Tex said, "I'll text her."

Tex did. We looked in the direction of the girls but saw nothing. Just as we began to turn our heads back around, one of the girls reached down for something. She positioned her cell phone in front of her and looked at it. With a smile on her face, she turned the cell to her friends. They leaned over and, while staring at the cell, they began to giggle. All three simultaneously turned their heads in our direction.

Tex was the first to raise his hand to wave at them. They waved back with thumbs-up gestures. I raised my hand in a waving motion, as did the Mackster and the Nose. Finally, Slo-Mo raised his hand while feeding his face the last of his hot dog with his other hand. We were on top of the world! The three-minute warning bell rang for class, so we gathered up our trash and trays. Tex let out a cowboy yell, "Yeeeeehawwwww!" We joined in as well.

After that, the Mackster asked Tex what it was that he texted to the girls.

"You mean Beth, Alexa, and Jezzie," said Tex.

"Yes," the Mackster said.

As he laughed, Tex shoved his cell phone in our faces while we read: *We think you're hot! What do you think about us?*

We all laughed and let out, in chorus, another cowboy yell as we left the cafeteria. "Yeeeehawwwww!"

Some Things to Think About

1. How is lunchtime at your school?

2. Is it hard to meet others, or are you like Tex?

3. Do you have a cell phone that you take to school?

4. What is your school's policy on cell phone use?

5. Have you ever texted something silly on your cell?

6. Has there ever been a time you wished you could retract something you sent from your cell to someone?

7. Cell phones are wonderful. Be cool, have fun, and use them wisely. What are your rules for good cell phone use?

Barbeque-Washers-Auctioneer

Some folks talk fast, and some folks talk slow.
On occasion, I say to both, "I can't understand you."

Just as Tex had promised, I received my invitation to attend a real family *Cowboy Barbeque* (BBQ) at his dad's ranch the following weekend. At the bottom, it read: *P.S. Bring extra clothes for an*

overnight campout after the BBQ is over and the other guests leave. I was psyched, and so were the rest of my buds.

It was Friday, the day of the BBQ. With our spirits high in anticipation of the campout on a *real* ranch, we all joked around the whole day at school. We didn't get much schoolwork accomplished. Besides, it was Friday. I had been to a little dude's day ranch a couple of years ago, but *this* was a dream come true. I thought how lucky I was to have good friends and a good friend like Tex too. I made sure that I issued a talkie to everyone and reminded them to have them turned on by arrival time at six o'clock.

My parents drove the five miles to the ranch grounds. A sign directed us to a place to park the car and wait. My dad seemed a little confused as to where to park. Mom then pointed and said to just find a place next to the other cars. We parked, and upon getting out, I noticed a cattle guard entrance that had a sign above it. As my dad read the sign, he turned to mom and said, "I'm sure the boys will have a fun time with that one." The sign read: The Double P Ranch.

Soon, two separate horse-drawn carriages arrived and were available to take us to the gathering place, which we could barely see in the distance. This was way too cool, I thought as I leaped into the carriage. I quickly retrieved my talkie and said, "This is Blake. Blake the Snake. Anybody got your ears on out there? Come on."

I got no answer, so I repeated, "Hey! This is the Snake. Anybody hear me? Come on back. Anybody? Anybody? Anybody I say."

To my surprise, a girl's voice came back over my talkie. The voice was breaking up, making it difficult to understand. I asked the person to identify herself. Next thing I heard was another voice that said, "This here's the Mackster. Whatcha got, good buddy."

"Hey, Mackster. It's Blake, and I'm on my way in. Who's that with you on the talkie?"

"Well, come on down, *pardner*. The other cowboys are all here waiting for ya, and there's plenty of grub to go around for all," the Mackster responded with a snicker. I then heard a girl's voice giggling in the background. The Mackster then said, "Oh yeah, that's Alexa you hear with me."

Surprised, I could only respond with a line I borrowed from the comedian and actor Jim Carey. "All righty then. Well, anyway ... I'll be right there."

"Take your time. Over and out," responded the Mackster.

"Take your time," I mused to myself. I then shouted to the carriage driver, "Can't this thing go any faster!"

My mom and dad, as well as Bengy, just turned and looked at me. I ignored them and focused my eyes on the slow-approaching gathering. We finally arrived, and Bengy bounded out of the carriage and said he was hungry and was heading for *the good stuff*. He stumbled upon hitting the ground and then caught himself to avoid falling. Dad reminded him to "meet back here at this spot no later than seven thirty" and then reemphasized with "not a minute later!"

Bengy's faded response was, "Watch that first step out of the carriage. It's a doozy." Then he added, "Sure, whatever you say, Dad."

Dad surveyed the crowd and commented, "There must be over 150 people here. Wow!"

Mom agreed without comment, but then she looked at dad and added, "It'll be fun. Let's go get something to eat before the line gets any longer. I'm hungry, and I don't have to cook or do the dishes!" And off they strolled as they told me to have a good time and said that they would be back tomorrow around ten o'clock to pick me up. I waved good-bye and walked over to where my buds were.

I greeted the Mackster and asked of Alexa's whereabouts. He responded that she only stopped by long enough to say hello and look at my talkie, and that was when I had called. He added, "Alexa told me to say hi to you."

It was a festive atmosphere I sensed as I greeted Tex. He high-fived us and said how he was glad to have us.

"Now, let's go get some *viddles* little doggies," Tex said as he shooed us along as if we were cattle.

"I can't wait for the campout," Slo- Mo said. We all nodded in agreement.

With very little conversation, we dug in and ate our fill … and more. Finally, the Nose exclaimed he couldn't eat another bite of brisket, sausage, or chicken, even if it were fed to him intravenously. At that point, Tex reminded everyone that there was banana pudding for dessert. The Nose was the first to head for the dessert line, and we all followed compliantly.

"Yippee ki-yay," the Mackster said. "This is the best pudding I've ever had. I think I'm gonna have seconds." We compliantly followed him for a second helping.

Have you ever seen the picture that has the monkeys with the big potbellies? One of the monkeys covers his eyes with his hands, another covers his mouth with his hands, and still another covers his ears with his hands. Well that would be a picture of the four of us with our bellies pouched out like the monkeys' bellies.

"We look like we're pregnant," I said disgustingly.

"*You* sure *do*," Tex replied.

This got a few chuckles from us. To change the subject, I told Tex that the music was great.

"Yes," he responded. "That's Alan Jackson singing now, Garth Brooks before him, and George Strait before Garth. Oh, and the Judds before George, and then of course there's Willie. My dad got that stereo system about two years ago specifically for outdoors."

I asked Tex how long had he lived here in California. He replied that this ranch was his grandfather's and that his dad was raised on it until he graduated from college, got married, and then moved to Houston, Texas.

"That's where I was born," Tex said with a big grin. "About two years ago, my grandparents were killed in a car accident. Our family came back for the funeral and never left. I've been here ever since. I love Houston, but I love it here too."

Turning around in his chair, he pointed and said, "Now, the stage that the stereo sits on was rented for *this* occasion. Shortly, we're going to turn off the music, and an auctioneer will come on and sell some antiques and things for a fundraiser," he said with his nose wrinkled. I asked Tex what the fundraiser was for, and he said it was for raising money for a monument in the city to honor the American Indians of this area. Other than that, he didn't know much more.

"But we don't have to hang around for that. Let's go to the washer pit and pitch a game of washers. I challenge you turkeys to a real man's game. Come on," Tex said as he skyrocketed up from his chair.

We followed suit while each of us bragged about how good we were at winning and how we were going to be *the* champion. Actually, none of us, except Tex, had ever played washers. It's a fun game I found out. It's a lot like pitching horseshoes, but instead of horseshoes being pitched, one pitches washers instead.

At twenty-one feet apart, two four-inch *cups* are placed flush into the ground. The metal washers are three inches across with a one-inch hole in the middle. These washers are tossed or hurled one at a time into the air from one end of the pit, or cup, and hopefully into the cup at the opposite end. Whoever gets the closest gets points each round until a winner is declared by reaching twenty-one points first.

We were having so much fun as we pitched washers and occasionally heard the auctioneer exclaim with a thunderous voice, "Sold!" At the conclusion of another game of washers, I looked down at my watch and realized that is was 8:03. I looked around and noticed that many of the guests had departed.

"Well, buckaroos," interrupted Tex, "the sun is setting low in the west, and darkness is approaching. It's time to get our backpacks and bags and head to the bunkhouse for the rest of the evening." And off we went as we followed Tex.

Some Things to Think About

1. Do you like cookouts?

2. Who does the cooking at cookouts in your family?

3. Have you ever eaten so much you were almost sick?

4. Have you been to an auction and heard an auctioneer? If so, did the auctioneer talk fast?

5. Have you ever tossed horseshoes or washers? If so, did you win?

The Campout

If a cowboy rode into town on Friday and left three days later on Friday, how the heck could that happen? Answer: The horse's name is Friday!

With bags in hand, we followed Tex a short distance. He dropped his bag, pointed, and declared, "Just past this small meadow and about a hundred yards or more past and beyond the tree line is where our campground and bunkhouse will be. Just follow and stay on the rabbit trails, and we'll be fine."

As we started on the trail, we came upon a sign that read: Don't Squat with Your Spurs On!

I heard Slo-Mo ask the Mackster, "What is that supposed to mean?"

"How am I supposed to know?" replied the Mackster.

Tex explained that his grandpa put these signs up a long time ago when his dad was a young'un.

A few steps later, we came across another sign that read: There's Two Theories to Arguing with a Woman—Neither One Works!

And another one that read: Never Kick a Fresh Cow Chip on a Hot Day!

"Now that one's funny," I said with laughter.

Not far, there was another sign that read: Never Hit a Man in the Mouth that Is Chewing Tobacco.

"That's even funnier," said Slo-Mo with a snicker. "And I get it!"

"Approaching another sign," said the Mackster. "I'll read it. *Never ask a barber if you need a haircut!*"

"I got the next one," said the Nose. *"Don't worry about bitin' off more than you can chew; your mouth is a whole lot bigger than you think!"*

"Hey, Tex," I said. "These are pretty cool signs. I like 'em. Your grandpa must have been an all right guy."

"Yes, sir, he was," responded Tex. "I always think of him when I see these signs and many other things around this ranch too. I have many fond memories visiting here from years past—Christmases, summer vacations, and the like.

"Oh, I got one for you," Tex blurted. "This is one my grandpa told me. If three cowboys are riding in a truck, how can you tell the real experienced cowboy from the other ones?"

We looked at each other in puzzlement and all responded in a matter-of-fact way that it couldn't be determined.

"Nonsense," said Tex. "The *real* experienced cowboy is the one in the middle! First thing is that he don't have to drive, and second is he don't have to open or otherwise mess with the gates, getting out and opening and closing them. The cowboy in the middle isn't there by mistake. Now that's cowboy logic!" Tex then let out a hearty "Yeeehaaawww!" After that, Tex said, "I got a million more of 'em. Just hang around, and I'll share them with you if you can stomach 'em." We laughed.

We stepped inside the tree line from the meadow, and wow, the tall trees provided a welcomed shade.

"Keep following the main animal trail," Tex reminded us, "and you'll be all right."

The trees and bushes were awesome. I slowed, stopped, and as I looked up, I could see the treetops swaying in the breeze. The light from the sun, what remained of it, glittered and danced across the tops of the tree leaves. Lost in this dream moment, I awoke to Tex calling out, "Come on, boys, keep up with me!"

Pushing the last of the tree limbs and brush aside, I followed Tex into an opening. This opening had a fire pit with several large rocks around it that looked like they had been used as chairs. A few seconds passed, and the Mackster stumbled in and fell upon one of the rock chairs.

"I'm exhausted," he said.

The Nose followed the Mackster's example, collapsed on another rock close by, and exclaimed, "Me too!"

Tex turned to me and held out his hands as if he were holding something in them. He pretended to be handing the make-believe something to the two of them, and then he made an announcement. "And this year, the Groaning Wimpy Award once again goes to the same ones that won it last year. May I present ..."

About that time, I interrupted and said, "Where's Slo-Mo?"

We all looked around, and the Nose slowly stated, "Beats me where he's at."

The Mackster then piped up with, "I'm too tired to care. Besides, he's always dragging in behind us, everywhere we go."

"That *is* true," the Nose said, "although he *was* first to get back in line for the banana pudding."

As we were conversing, Tex let out a big ole yell that went something like this: "Kippy ki-yo, little Slo-Mo! It's time for you to come home. We're over here, little doggie."

The rest of us sat looking at each other and wondering if Tex thought he was magic and could somehow make Slo-Mo appear. Well, I'm here to tell you that within two minutes Slo-Mo sleepily staggered into the camp. It seemed to me as if Slo-Mo had just woken up. The Nose spoke up and said, "You been crying. You got lost, and you've been crying. I know it!"

Slo-Mo just stared at the Nose and declared, "No. No I haven't."

"Sure enough, I can tell," said the Nose.

"Don't think so," said Tex with conviction. "He's late 'cause he was chasing that illusive squirrel I've been trying to catch for some time. I saw him a ways back split off, chasing it. That's why he's late. Right, Slo-Mo?"

"That's right, and he's a fast one too," replied Slo-Mo.

"Now, enough of this," Tex said. "Let's get unpacked and settled in. We can sleep outdoors, here in the pit area, or inside in the bunkhouse. As for me, I'm sleeping inside, as I hear it's supposed to get down to the upper forty degrees tonight. Kind of nice right now though." Tex rubbed his hands together.

We threw some logs in the fire pit along with sticks we had gathered. It was burning good now, and our beds were ready for us when we'd be ready for them … but not yet. I noticed Slo-Mo and Tex over by themselves talking while the rest of us were warming ourselves by the fire and roasting marshmallows. I'm not sure what they were talking about, but I imagine the conversation went something like this:

Slo-Mo: "Thanks, Tex, for hollowing real loud. I was feeling lost after chasing after and then losing that squirrel. I got all turned around, and there were several trails to choose from. I didn't know which one to follow. When I heard you holler, it made me realize I wasn't too far off, and so I just began walking in the direction of your voice. Thanks again."

Tex: "No problem. It's happened to me a time or two. I just did what my dad did when it happened to me."

Slo-Mo: "Well, thanks again."

Tex: "You're welcome."

Some Things to Think About

1. When was the last time you went on a campout? Well, that's too long!

2. Have you ever built a fire?

3. Have you ever roasted marshmallows? If so, how many did you eat?

4. Have you ever gotten lost or do you know someone who has? If you got lost, how did you find your way back? How did you feel when you found your way back?

The Ghost in the Dark
that Wanders

Champions come and go, but I'll be staying awhile.

It was dark now. We were taking turns playing thumb wars by the fire pit. The others were out of the game, as they had already lost three times each. The championship was between me and the Nose. We clasped our hands with our fingers interlocked. In anticipation, we lifted our thumbs. Without blinking, we glared into each other's eyes. The Mackster shouted, "Go!" Twenty seconds later, the Nose was declared the winner.

"It's not fair!" I shouted. "His nose was in the way, and … and … it breathed on me!" I complained playfully. "I could have won. I could have been the winner, I know it! But no, you ... you and your nose ruined everything for me," I jovially continued.

"Save it for the acting class," the Nose said.

With his finger, the Nose pointed to his nose, tilted his head in my direction, and stated, "Always remember that the Nose knows. And it knows all things, especially how to win at thumb wars!" Laughter engulfed him as he walked away and slapped the Mackster on the back. I turned the other way while shooing him away with my hand.

Out of the corner of my eye, I noticed that Tex wasn't paying attention to us but was fixed on something out in the darkness. I called out to him, "What are you looking at?" He, in a crab-like walk, headed closer to me.

"I've got a confession about this area to tell you," Tex said in a low voice as all eyes focused on him. "About a century ago, the legend tellers say, a young Indian boy and girl fell in love. Although they were from the same tribe, the parents were not on good terms with one another due to some unknown distant dispute. The youths were responsible for obtaining water for their respective families from a nearby river. When they could, they would time their water retrieving and meet by the river to enjoy each other's company. This continued for a while, but then suspicions arose."

Tex continued as our eyes departed not away from him. "On this one occasion, they met as usual. They walked, talked, they strolled, and they even danced a dance. Time got away as they realized that darkness had covered the land. Suddenly, a rustling noise was heard in the nearby bushes. The young Indian brave cautiously approached the bush, but the noise was not to be heard again. The brave turned to find his girl, but she was nowhere to be found. It is said that the young brave wanders these parts searching for her and calling out her name. Her first name was Banana, but he called her by a name he affectionately gave her, and that name was Pudding. To this day, they haunt the places where Banana Pudding is being served. They especially haunt those who eat too much of it. Wait! ...What is that?"

Tex pointed into the dark brush and declared, "It's her! She's over there!"

We all quickly stood up and looked in the direction Tex was pointing in. Something glowing was approaching. Just as soon as we saw the glow, a human figure approached. It was the form of a woman all right. We heard a voice that sent us scrambling. Dust filled the air, as fast wasn't fast enough for us to vacate the area. Stumbling and bumping into each other was bad enough, but not as bad as if we didn't get out of there.

I refocused my eyes, and through the dust I saw a woman. The woman was standing next to Tex ... and they were laughing. We slowly, and somewhat confused and maybe a little embarrassed, looked around. Out from the bushes I emerged while the others slowly came out from behind the chair rocks. Tex looked at us and then stepped forward.

"Boys, I'd like for you to meet my mom, Mrs. Strait," Tex said, grinning.

"Hi, boys," said Mrs. Strait. "I see Wesley is telling his tall tales again. I do hope you all are having a good time, and we're *so* glad to have you here."

"Wesley? Oh yeah, that's Tex," I reminded myself.

"Gather around and don't be shy, boys," Mrs. Strait encouraged. "I brought you all a little light snack of the leftovers from the barbeque. See, some more good ole banana pudding. I texted Wesley and told him I was coming with this pudding. You did get the message, didn't you?"

Some Things to Think About

1. Do you have a favorite dessert? If so, what is it?

2. Do you have a storyteller in your family? If so, who is it?

3. Do you have a best scary story? Write or tell it!

How High Is the Moon?

You can't do nothing <u>after</u> midnight
that you can't do <u>before</u> midnight.

With our bellies full of pudding, four of us lay on the ground as Tex vanished into the bushes to take a wiz. We had restroom facilities in the bunkhouse, but what the hey, we did what boys do in these circumstances of the great outdoors. Contented, the rest of us had our faces pointed upward and fixed on the stars.

We talked of the immensity of space and pondered where did it all end and what was after that. Pointing toward the night sky, we located a couple of the constellations and felt very satisfied that we had.

The Nose turned to me and said, "I'm going to tell you a story, but you have to participate in it. Okay?"

"Okay," I said.

"I'm going to tell you a story about a cow. After I finish it, I'm going to say, 'I one it,' and then you'll say, 'I two it,' and then we'll continue on back and forth like that. You got it?"

"I got it," I replied.

The Nose began by saying, "I was out in the countryside walking along a fence one day when I came upon an old dead cow. It had maggots crawling in it, and it looked terrible. Horrible as it was, I claimed it and said, 'I one it.' ... Hey, it's your turn."

"Oh, yeah. I forgot. What was I supposed to say," I inquired.

"I two it," he repeated softly.

"Oh yeah, I two it," I said.

"I three it," he returned.

"I four it," I returned back.

"I five it," he said.

"I six it. Is this going anywhere?" I said.

"I seven it. Just keep going," the Nose said.

"I eight it," I said.

"Ha! Ha! Ha! You ate it. You ate the old dead cow!" the Nose shouted as the others joined in with his laughter.

I gave them my meanest disgusted look I could come up with, but it didn't seem to alter their almost horizontal position from laughter one iota. I determined that I would get back at the Nose. I would be patient and wait for the right opportunity ... and then Tex emerged from the bushes.

"What's all the noise?" Tex asked.

In my eagerness, I blurted out, "Nothing. Come on over and join us. Say, Tex, I've got a game to play, and it takes two to play it."

"I love games," Tex said. "I'll play."

"Good. It goes like this. I'm going to tell a story about a cow. After I finish it, I'm going to say, 'I one it,' and then you'll say, 'I two it,' and then we'll continue on back and forth like that. You got it?"

"I got it," he replied.

I then began by saying, "I was out in the countryside walking along a fence one day when I came upon an old dead cow. It had maggots crawling in it, and it looked terrible. Horrible as it was, I claimed it and said, 'I one it.' ... Hey, now it's your turn."

"I two it," Tex said.

I turned to the others and said, "Ummm, Tex is catching on faster than I thought he would. I three it."

"I four it," he said.

"I five it," I said with a grin.

"I six it," He said.

"I seven it," I said as my grin grew bigger. I then looked around at my other buds and, one by one, gave them a nod that said, "I'm going in for the kill now."

With laughter and a pointing finger, Tex said, "I jumped *over* the fence, and *you* ate it!"

Only humiliation can describe what I felt as laughter that originated from a bunch of dimwits filled the air and touched the stars. The moon seemed to be laughing too.

Tex quickly regained himself and said, "Don't feel too bad, Blake ole boy. I've heard that one before, and I fell for it the first time I heard it too."

In the distance, we were startled by a noise. "What was that?" we asked.

"It's a rooster," stated Tex. "Sun should be coming up shortly."

All of us pulled our wrists to our faces and declared the time to be five o'clock. Looking at each other with droopy eyes, we silently walked to the bunkhouse and slipped into our beds. Within two minutes, I was sound asleep. Later, I awoke about nine o'clock to the aroma of bacon and eggs cooking, with the added smell of toast.

"Up and at 'em, boys," declared Mr. and Mrs. Strait. "We decided to join you fellers for a hearty breakfast before your parents come for you."

I didn't want to get up, but the aroma was too welcoming not to. Getting up and having a good meal in our stomachs gave us a new spurt of energy. That didn't last very long, as my parents arrived soon thereafter. On the drive back with my parents to the house, I went back to sleepy land and stayed there till the next morning.

Some Things to Think About

1. Do you know a good joke?

2. Tell a joke to a friend.

3. Have you ever had a prank pulled on you? Tell about it.

4. Have you ever pulled a prank on someone? Tell about it.

5. Could you ever be a stand-up comedian?

6. Try telling two jokes to your class or add some jokes in a paper you have to write to make it more enjoyable to read.

Alan ... the Car Guy

Alan is my name ... cars are my game.

"Monday is already here," I said as I sat in English class. In timid anticipation, I looked around at my classmates. *Who is going to be next?* I silently asked myself. This was something I hated—presenting a report to the class.

"Alan McFee. You're next. Come on down," said Ms. Simpson.

Alan quickly rose up only to stumble as he headed to the front of the room and the podium. After the laughter subsided, I reminded myself that was something I had to remember not to do when it was my turn. He sure seemed nervous, but when he opened his mouth, it all went away. As he began, I became very interested in what he had to say. "My great-grandfather was an automobile worker in Detroit, Michigan, for forty years," Alan said. "When he was very young and had just started working for the auto company, he met Mr. Ford. Mr. Ford came around and visited the auto plant, shook everyone's hand, and thanked them for the great work they were engaged in.

"He told them how he appreciated working with them in this great endeavor and for the great American future. Mr. Ford said, 'Someday, almost everyone will own and operate a car.' I think he was right!

"Yes, he was right, as this is the year 2013, and my parents have a car, and so does almost everyone I know. I like cars, and I collect miniature ones. I have in my collection over four hundred of them, and I have them displayed all around my bedroom. I sleep on sheets, a blanket, and a comforter that have car imprints all over them.

"My bed is a car bed; I love sleeping in it. At the foot of my bed is a big box that I keep my important things in. The box has writing on it. In real big letters, it has *Tool Box* on the side. I have other things in my room too. My room has many posters of cars. The first car my dad owned was a 1964 Ford Falcon Futura. The car was white with red interior and had bucket seats. It also had chrome wheels. One of my posters is of this car among the many others. You've probably guessed what my favorite movie is.

"My favorite movie is *Cars*. I've watched it thirty-four times. My most favorite birthday party was when I was in the second grade and my parents threw me a car party. We had a game where we told each other about our most favorite car, and then we watched the movie *Cars*. All seven of us watched while sitting on my car beanbag chairs. We drank from glasses that were shaped like car pistons, and we ate my birthday cake that was shaped like a car. We loved it!

"The following week, our class went to the library. The library lady sat us on the carpet squares. We sat down, and I forgot I had one of my small toy cars in my hand. She reminded me that I needed to put it away in my pocket, so I did.

"The library lady asked who had a birthday recently. I raised my hand. I told her and my class about my birthday party. The library lady said she had a special book to read to us that today.

"Because it was the month that my birthday was in, she read about cars and the different colors and sizes they come in. It was a special trip to the library for me, and the library lady made it special by reading her book about cars. After she read the car book, she allowed me to get my car out from my pocket and tell the class about it, and I did."

"Thank you, Alan," said Ms. Simpson. "Do I have a volunteer to be next or will I need to call on someone?"

Some Things to Think About

1. Do you have a hobby like Alan?

2. What kind of a vehicle does your family have?

3. What color is your family car, or is it a truck?

4. Is your car or truck really small or really big?

5. Have you ever gone on a long trip in your vehicle? If so, where did you go on your trip?

Library Day-Yeah!

Reading is fun! Would you like to read with me?

As Alan finished his presentation, it reminded me of my elementary school days and especially of my fond library times. I can still recall those good ole days like they were yesterday.

"Hurray! It's library time," we would all shout as Ms. Rodriquez lined the class up at the door. Ms. Rodriquez didn't even ask us to be quiet, as she liked our enthusiasm about reading and going to the library. She did, however, remind us to be sure we had our library books to turn in and to be quiet in the hallway going to the library.

We would line up out in the hall very quietly. Our hands were placed behind our backs, we had *bubbles* in our mouth, and our line was very straight. The line stayed straight all the way down and into the library. Each of us in turn took our spot on the checkered and multi-colored carpet. We all sat *crisscross applesauce* and were very quiet. We all knew our assigned color spot, and our librarian, Ms. Gonzales, sat down in a chair in front. She had some books in her lap.

Ms. Gonzales showed us three books. One book was about animals, the next one was about various kinds of fish, and the last one was about different plants. She told us a quick summary about each one. She knew how to talk to us and tell us very interesting stories.

As I looked around the library area, I noticed colorful yellow bookshelves along the three walls with windows above them. A fourth red bookshelf divided the area we were in from the rest of the main library area. The bookshelves were only about four feet high and had many things sitting on top of them.

One bookshelf had a cat with a really tall, red, and white hat on his head. The cat also had a red bow tied around his neck. This cat was next to a lamp shaped like a hand, and the hand was holding up the lamp with a lampshade. The lampshade was shaped like a hat and was also very tall. It had the same color and design of the hat that the cat had on.

The next thing I recall was a monkey. The monkey was brown with a yellow stomach, and he had a yellow and red knit cap on his head. At the top of the cap was a little, fuzzy, round, green ball-looking thing. He also had a nicely knitted scarf around his neck. The scarf was also yellow and red but didn't have any green on it. This monkey looked very relaxed as he was sitting and leaning against a palm tree. I sure wished I could be leaning against that tree with him!

On another shelf was a big—and I really do mean a *big*, red dog. The dog had a black collar around his neck. He also had big, black eyes and a big, black nose. This dog had a big, red bowl that was full of dog food sitting in front on him, and it was mostly eaten up. The big, red dog was lying in his doghouse with his head sticking out. The doghouse looked like it was too little for him.

Next to the big, red dog was an odd-looking guy with big, round, black-rimmed glasses. But he was kind of cool too. He had on blue cargo shorts with a brown pullover sweater and a light yellow, collared shirt underneath. His ears, instead of being on the side of his head, were on top of his head. He sort of looked like a rabbit but also like a mouse, or maybe a little bit like a kangaroo. I asked the librarian what he was, and she said she thought he was an aardvark. "Well," I told her, "I guess so since I haven't seen too many of them." In fact, I don't recall ever seeing a real aardvark.

After that, a really cool-looking cat caught my eye. This cat had orange fur with some black marks on his back side. His eyelids covered most of his eyes, and he looked lazy and relaxed at the same time. He had really big paws, and he also had a sneaky look about him. He didn't look like the kind of cat that had *ever* caught a mouse. He just didn't look like he could or would want to run that fast!

The next figure I saw was a boy about my age. When I looked into his eyes, he reminded me of myself. He wore a yellow, or maybe it was a gold, shirt with black zigzags going around the middle. He wore black shorts and brown shoes. He only had a little bit of hair. In the middle of his shirt was the name "Charlie." I wanted my mom to buy me a shirt with my name on it too.

Another one was a figure of a boy sitting down. He had on a red shirt with three small, black stripes going around it. He looked very small and was sucking his thumb. He had a blue, kind of dirty blanket he was holding very close to him. His hair was scraggly looking. He was holding his blanket so tightly that I don't think anyone could get it from him. He made me feel big, as I remembered that when I was younger, I too used to do things like that.

Toward the end of the library visit, the librarian would call for us to turn in our library books so we could check out some more books. I recall searching for a special book that I hadn't found yet. Then, to my surprise, I halted!

This one looks pretty good, I thought to myself.

My mind flashed back to my best friend at the time. His name was Jay. He had showed and told me about the book, as he had been reading it—at least I thought it was the same one. I picked it up and declared, "Yep, it has a wimpy boy on the cover just like I remembered. This is the one all right."

"Ms. Gonzales, this is the book I'd like to check out," I proudly announced.

"Blake … Blake Sloan," said Ms. Simpson. "For the third time, it's time to give your report."

Some Things to Think About

1. Why do you go to the library?

2. Do you remember your last trip to the library?

3. What rules do you have to follow when going to, inside, and from the library?

4. What books do you like?

5. What was the last book you checked out at the library?

6. What is your favorite book?

7. Do you have any thoughts about what the next book you'll read will be?

Choosing Bob

Do you make your own decisions or do you let others make them for you?

"Yes, Ms. Simpson. I know it's my turn to give my report. I'll be right up," I said without much enthusiasm. I then added under my breath, "Sixth grade isn't much fun."

I reminded myself not to stumble like Alan did earlier. I could feel sweat building up on my forehead. I felt like I had just eaten a hot pepper. I pushed myself out of my seat, took a step, and ... stumbled. *Dab blast it, I wasn't supposed to do that*, I thought. I regained my footing and pressed forward. As I got to the front, I turned to face the class and ... stumbled again.

"Go ahead, Blake, if you're ready," Ms. Simpson encouraged.

Ms. Simpson's voice was so very encouraging that I forgot about being nervous, and then I began.

"My report is about a friend named Bob that I once knew when I was in the fourth grade. He has since moved to Las Vegas, and he told me this story about something that happened to him about a year before he told it to me. I will present my report as if I were Bob. I will now begin.

"Hello, my name is Bob. You know me. I'm the kid that gets chosen last when picking sides on the playground for games. All through kindergarten, also the first grade, and the first half of second grade, it was the same story—last one chosen. But that changed when a new kid moved in from another town from New Mexico. His name was Doyce.

"I'd never heard a name like that, but then I had never met a kid like him either. He wasn't real short, and he wasn't real tall; he was just average. He had reddish-brown hair, and his eyes were blue. He wasn't real skinny, and he wasn't real fat; he was just average. But when I think about him, he's anything but average to me.

"First time I met him was on the playground during recess. He was one grade older than me, and he was appointed by our PE coach, Coach Littlefield, to be one of the two playground captains for that week. That meant he would get to pick sides for the games we would play for that day. Third-graders got to do that sort of thing, and it was something we second-graders got to look forward to.

"The game for the day was going to be indoor soccer. We all lined up, and I took my usual place, which was toward the end, and I took a step back so that when I was chosen last it wouldn't be too obvious. But unknown to me, this day was going to be different. After the two captains stepped out front and took their places, they called out names, and those chosen stepped toward and then behind their captain. And then it happened.

"About halfway through the picking of players, I looked up and saw Doyce looking my way. I quickly turned away. I looked up again, and he was still looking. Two other guys were standing next to him, leaning over, and whispering in his ear. I barely heard one say, 'Don't pick him.' Once again I looked away and waited for the next person to be called. I heard a name.

"'Bob, Bob White.' I didn't move. It had to be a mistake. I made that mistake last year, and it created my *most embarrassing moment* ever. But this time I heard my name clearly for the *second time*. 'Bob, I chose you,' said the voice again, and it came from Doyce. It was no mistake! I walked to the players' line and repeated to myself several times, 'I wasn't chosen last.' I got behind Doyce and the others; I felt like I was accepted for the first time.

"Well, fate stepped in that day. Our team was tied 3–3 with fifteen seconds left on the running clock. Rudy kicked a long flying ball in the air that came in my direction. The soccer ball came in my sight from my left side and was curving to my right side. I made the turn and got ready to kick, but the soccer ball continued soaring and going higher than I thought, so I kept backing up. The next thing I recall was the feeling of the ball bouncing off of my head. It was the soccer ball all right, and then I saw the most beautiful thing happen. I saw the ball float just over the outstretched hands of the goalie and into the goalie net.

"'Score!' called out the coach. Then he blew his whistle and announced, 'Game over. Doyce's team wins, thanks to Bob using his head.' The teams on both sides burst out with laughter, but *I, yes I,* laughed the loudest. From that day on, I was never chosen last ever again."

"Well, thank you, Blake, for that inspiring story," announced Ms. Simpson.

"Oh, I'm not finished yet," I told Ms. Simpson.

"Oh, please, go ahead and finish," she said.

"Well, I just wanted to conclude my report on this added note: Bob was so happy that during art class he drew a picture of his soccer team with him making the winning goal. He took the picture home that day and showed it to his parents. That night, just before he went to sleep, he taped it above his bed. He slept very well that night.

"And I say good for you, and way to go, Bob!"

"Very good," said Ms. Simpson. "Tomorrow we'll finish up. For now, we will dismiss at the bell ... and there it is now."

Some Things to Think About

1. Were you happy for Bob?

2. What are your thoughts concerning Doyce?

3. Could you make a decision like Doyce did even when others want you to make a different decision?

4. Tell your school class, a friend, a brother or sister, or your parents about a similar situation you have had.

5. What did Bob mean when he said he thought that Doyce was *not* an average kid?

6. Do you have a hero in your life? If so, who is your hero? Tell someone about your hero.

Show and Tell

Have you ever tried to surprise someone, and you ended up being the one surprised?

It was Ricky's turn to give his report. *Poor guy*, I thought. *I'm just glad mine is over.* I was so relaxed. Ricky squared himself in front of the class, and I said in a supportive voice, "Do it, Ricky. Get 'er done!"

Ricky gave me and the class a big thumbs-up as Ms. Simpson gave the go ahead. I learned some things about Ricky that I hadn't previously known.

"I grew up in Los Angeles, California, until I reached the fourth grade," Ricky began. "We then moved to a small rural town named Elida, New Mexico. I didn't fit in at first. I was city all over, and this place was country through and through. But after a week of school, I met Steve. He had been out sick for a few days and showed up on Monday with his big ranch hat, jeans, and the funniest smile on his face I ever saw. I don't ever recall him not smiling now that I think about it. I believe his smile was just part of his face *all* of the time.

"I was out on the playground during recess, and it was he that came up and asked me to join him in basketball with the other boys. It was a welcomed invitation, which I quickly accepted. He wasn't that good at basketball, but he sure was funny when he had the ball, which made everyone laugh.

"One time I remember he and Ron bounced the basketball back and forth to each other using their heads. Then after six times back and forth like that, Steve turned around and bounced the ball off of his butt, and the ball went up into the air and *almost* made it into the basketball net. Basketball players they were *not,* but *clowns* they were, and we were becoming good friends. I missed my friends in Los Angeles, but I was making new ones there in New Mexico.

"During English class, Ms. Newman gave us an assignment. This coming Friday was to be our *Show and Tell* time. She explained that this time occurred often at the lower elementary grades but only on occasion in her class, and this was one of those occasions. She said she had a surprise for the best and most original presentation. She said, 'Be prepared and surprise me!'

"I was really beginning to like this school and the orderly way in which Ms. Newman organized her classroom. It was student friendly. On all of the desks were placed and taped down three cards. At the upper left corner of the each desk was a green card that read *I got it*, in the upper middle of the desk was a yellow card that read *I'm thinking*, and finally at the far right was a card that read *I need help!* We just pointed to the card that fit our need as she walked over to check on us.

"Well, Friday came, and we were in our morning class, with Ms. Newman preparing us for *Show and Tell*. However, someone was missing, and that someone was Steve. But then he stumbled in with his long and loud smile. He bent over and whispered something in Ms. Newman's ear. Ms. Newman cleared her throat and announced that we would begin our *Show and Tell* time and that Steve would start us off.

"Steve took his spot in front of the class. For the first time, I noticed the usual large smile was missing from his face. He walked over and opened the classroom door and led in a plump sheep that, he explained, came from his father's ranch. My mouth must have been open during his entire presentation. This would not have happened in any of my classes in Los Angeles. I kept looking at the teacher and thinking she was going to stop Steve and make him get rid of the animal and then send him to the principal's office, but she didn't. And I'm glad she didn't because I learned a lot about sheep during Steve's short presentation. *He's going to win*, I thought to myself. But he didn't.

"Well, Ms. Newman was choosing students randomly, and after thirty minutes went by, my name was called. I took my place after I got my cage with Taco in it from behind the closet door. I introduced Taco to the class and said he was my pet rat. I gave my presentation on rats in general for about five minutes, and I could detect that the class was very quiet. I felt they didn't like my presentation, and so at my closing remarks, I ended by saying, "And I don't give a *flip* if you like Taco, my presentation, or me ... but *I* do."

An unexpected and weird thing happened at my closing statement. Just as I said the word *flip*, Taco eased up on his hind legs, turned a summersault flip, and landed back down on *all fours*. I was totally surprised, as it sent up a humorous roar with applause across the classroom. At the end of *Show and Tell*, I was awarded the prize for the Best Show and Tell, not just for the day, but 'ever,' to quote Ms. Newman.

"And that, I tell my friends on Facebook, is how I got the nickname of Ricky the Rat."

"Wow," I said to Ricky as he took his seat next to mine. "Did that really happen?"

"Well, that's my story, and I'm sticking to it," he said with a smile.

"Next," said Ms. Simpson as she looked at Skylar.

"Yes, Ms. Simpson," replied Skylar.

Some Things to Think About

1. Do you have a pet? If so, what is the name of your pet? Can your pet do a trick?

2. Have you ever had to move to a different school?

3. Tell about one of your *Show and Tell* stories.

Snowy Weather for Skylar

Did you ever have so much fun that it hurt?

"We will now hear from our new student, who moved here just last week," Ms. Simpson informed us. "Go ahead, Skylar."

"Hello, I'm Skylar, and I'm going to tell you about Alaska, as that is where I was born.

"Living in Alaska is cold and snowy, but we sure have lots of fun playing outside in it. 'You have to be careful,' Grandma would always caution us, 'because if it gets too cold, you might freeze, and then I'd have to get all bundled up, and then I would have to go out into the cold, drag you back into the cabin, and put you by the fireplace to get you thawed out! That would be a hassle, so don't stay out too long.' Grandma was odd yet *cool* that way.

"Grandma was born in 1952. She would tell us about the *good old days* and the fond memories she had from her younger years. When she was growing up in *the village*, many still had dogs that pulled a sled to get around from village to village in the smaller communities. 'Some still do to this day,' she would add. Today, most use snowmobiles instead of the dog and sled to get around in the villages. Back then, like today, it was very important to know the weather forecast of the area, as it could be a matter of a life or death situation.

"So when the villagers talk about the cold weather, it was and still is in terms of how many dogs are going to be needed to pull the sled for traveling that evening and into the night. If mild weather was to be expected and only one dog was needed to pull the sled, then it is referred to as a *one-dog night*. If the weather is a bit colder, then two dogs might be needed, and it is referred to as a *two-dog night*. If colder than that, it would be a *three-dog night*, and it would be continued in that manner.

"A rock group from the 1960s took their name from this idea, Grandma told us. They called themselves *Three Dog Night*, and they had numerous hit songs and were very popular during that time. I like their songs, even today, as grandma plays her sixties music and tells us interesting stories and facts like that and about her growing-up years.

"Last year, my little sister, Melissa, and I played outside with the other neighborhood children. It started out with only my sister and me throwing snowballs at each other. Within five minutes, all the kids in our area joined in on the snowball fun. After a while, our grandma poked her head out from the front door and reminded us we needed to come in real soon and warm up. We ignored her. We were having too much fun.

"We were having too much fun all right, but that didn't last much longer as our toes began to become number than they already were. We walked to the front door as if we were icicles—frozen and stiffened up. Our feet and toes were not just *numb,* they began to hurt as we began to warm up. Grandma was right; we stayed out too long in the cold.

"But Grandma knew what to do. She had a nice warm bath prepared. After we were all dried off and had fresh clothes on, she served us cookies and milk. She turned our cold hurt into a cozy, warm feeling. My grandma is the smartest and the greatest ever. I hope you have a nice grandma, as nice as mine."

"Thank you, Skylar. We're out of time and still have seven students who need to give their report," announced Ms. Simpson. "That's okay, though. Have a great Thanksgiving holiday, and those seven, be prepared to give your reports the Monday we come back. Happy Thanksgiving!"

Some Things to Think About

1. Why does Skylar call her grandma odd and also cool?

2. Do you like to play in the snow? If so, what kind of games do you play in the snow?

3. Have you ever built a snow person?

4. Have you ever ridden on a snowmobile?

5. Would you like to visit Alaska?

6. Can you find Alaska on a map? Can you find your state you live in?

Thanksgiving Day

Thank you for Thanksgiving!

Thanksgiving Day at my house is the best! Yes, school is out for a precious few days, and I already smell the pies being prepared for the Thanksgiving holiday. Grandma said she was preparing her favorite pie, pecan. Mom is in the process of preparing her favorite, pumpkin. I like them both. Uncle Jason and Aunt Leela brought the dressing, and Uncle Bill and Aunt Betty just walked in with a great big bowl of pistachio fruit salad. Ummm. Ummm. Ummm.

All my cousins are here too. We like to play hide and seek. Last year, I hid in the dirty clothes basket. I got in the bottom of the basket and piled the dirty clothes on top of me. After a while, I fell asleep. None of my cousins could find me, so everyone started looking for me, even the adults. My grandpa finally found me. The reason he found me is because he said that happened to him once when he was young, and that was the very same place he hid too.

Grandpa had on his tuxedo shirt, the one grandma told him not to wear, but he wore it anyway. Grandma wore her turkey shirt, the one grandpa told her not to wear, but she did anyway. I think they wore them to annoy each other. They do things like that and then laugh about it. They're fun grandparents.

Aunt Leela keeps singing Christmas songs, and we keep reminding her that this is Thanksgiving time, *not* Christmas. Aunt Betty just dyed her hair orange for the holiday. We call her pumpkin head. When we call her pumpkin head, she sticks her tongue out at us, and we then run away from her and out into the backyard.

The backyard is where Uncles Jason and Bill hang out with my dad. The reason they stay out there is so they won't get in the way of the *Kitchen Queens*. The Kitchen Queens are the "women folk,' they say. They like us running around in the backyard so we can go and get them their sodas to drink and snacks to eat. But I must warn you about Uncle Jason. He has a nickname, and his nickname is *Stinky*, and there is a very good reason for that nickname.

My mom likes crafts, and so she gathers me and all my cousins around the kitchen table in the morning on Thanksgiving Day. We cut out and color Thanksgiving Day turkeys. After we're finished, she collects them and puts them on the big dinner table for decorations while we eat *the big* Thanksgiving Day dinner. Even Bengy helped with the turkey decorations. Mom told him if he didn't help, then he couldn't have any dessert.

My dad and the uncles decided to deep fry our turkey this year. So back in the backyard, we had to be careful not to knock over or otherwise run into the cooking setup they had for deep frying the turkey. But they kept us busy getting them drinks, chips, and snacks from the kitchen.

I must go now because it is time to eat. Oh, yeah, I'm not sitting next to Stinky, I mean Uncle Jason, this year. If he ever asks you to pull his finger, please don't, because if you do, you'll be sorry. Remember, you've been warned. Happy Thanksgiving!

Some Things to Think About

1. What is your favorite food at Thanksgiving time?

2. Is your family like this one? If so, in what ways?

3. How do you like your turkey cooked?

4. What is your favorite dessert?

5. Do you like pumpkin or pecan pie the best?

6. Is it usually cold or warm outside at Thanksgiving where you live?

Dancing Ants!

I won't tell on you if you won't tell on me.

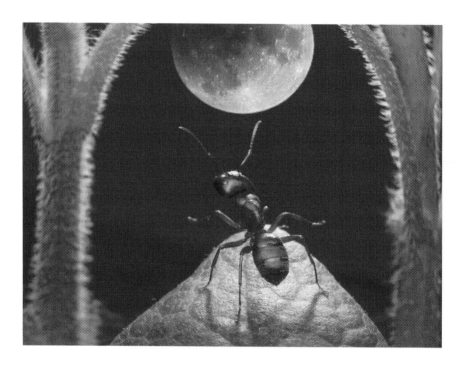

Ugh, back in school. Actually, if truth be told, the stories had perked an interest in me. I was getting to know more about my friends than I previously knew. The story about Ricky and his rat reminded me of an ant story that happened to me in the first grade. It goes like this:

There I was sitting outside the principal's office. Ms. Morgan sent me there for something the other kids said I did while Ms. Morgan was out of the classroom. It all started while we were in reading circle, and Ms. Morgan was reading to us. She was midway through reading *The Little Engine that Could* when another teacher from across the hall opened the door and asked to speak to her. Ms. Morgan excused herself and told us to be on our best behavior, and then she put Elizabeth in charge as she stepped just outside the classroom with Ms. Charles.

We *were* on our best behavior. *None* of us made a sound. But then something happened. We couldn't hear Ms. Morgan and Ms. Charles talking anymore. George got up the nerve and quietly, very quietly, got up from his seat and slowly, very slowly, walked to the door. He stuck his head out from the door and turned around and said to the rest of us, "They're gone all the way to the end of the hallway." George then made a snickering grin.

That was our cue that things were about to change as George did his spider walk across the floor and back to his chair. Not to be out done, Vincent made a gurgling sound with his throat. He did this several times. Sue sat in her seat and began tapping one of her chair legs with her foot. Mary and Jolyne began talking, and Ramos began to sing.

From the other side of the room, Carl and Nancy held hands and swung their clasped hands back and forth. Josh and Hector thought it was recess and began chasing each other around the room and almost knocked over the world globe that was on Ms. Morgan's desk. That sent a united *ooooohhh* sound throughout the class. It did quiet us down, but only for a few seconds. And then it all started up again, but this time with more noise than before.

Elizabeth stood up and declared through her black-rimmed glasses, "You better behave or I'm gonna tell!"

Billy then mimicked Elizabeth. "You better behave or I'm—"

He abruptly stopped as Elizabeth stood over him and stared him to silence.

It was too much for me. I couldn't let Ramos and the rest have all the attention. Finally, I jumped up out of my chair and ran into the middle of the reading circle and shouted, "You want to dance? I got ants in my pants!" That sent a roar of laughter from the classroom, which went out and into the hall. Shortly afterward, the laughter died down, and we could hear footsteps coming down the hallway. These were not just anybody's footsteps; these particular footsteps belonged to Ms. Morgan. We could tell.

As soon as the footsteps stopped, our eyes were focused on the door of our classroom. Yes, Ms. Morgan entered, and as soon as she walked in, Elizabeth jumped up and said, "I told you all to be quiet and now I'm going to tell!"

Sure, I thought. *She can't tell on all of us with all the things the whole class did.* But I was wrong.

Elizabeth then pointed her evil finger my way and said, "That guy, Blake, was dancing in the middle of the reading circle and made everyone laugh. He said, 'You wanna dance? I got ants in my pants.'"

I recall shrinking back down into my chair. That lasted only a few seconds, as Ms. Morgan firmly took hold of my hand and escorted me out of the class and toward the principal's office. I had never been to the principal's office before. I started to sweat. After I sat down outside the principal's office, the nervous sweat stopped, but I still was not very relaxed. So there I sat waiting to see Mr. Boganeto.

I don't recall ever going *into* the principal's office that day. Maybe he was out, or maybe Ms. Morgan never intended for me to see him but just wanted to use me to set an example or send a message to rest of the class. Certainly she couldn't and wouldn't tolerate the unruly behavior of the class when she was gone that time. Somehow I think she knew about the whole class's behavior; teachers are funny that way. I really don't know how she knew, 'cause I didn't tell.

Some Things to Think About

1. What do you think Blake would have told the principal?

2. What would you have told the principal?

3. How *should* one act if a teacher is out of the classroom?

4. Why did Elizabeth tell on only Blake?

5. Should everyone that acted up be punished, or only the ones that misbehaved the most?

6. Tell about one good behavior you have done this week.

May I Introduce
Mr. Kilgore ... Your Sub

I like to meet new people. I also like my old friends.

On Wednesday, I met Mr. Kilgore. Our regular science teacher, Ms. Bopart, was gone because she had an appointment at the dentist's office. Her tooth started hurting after lunch on Monday. I heard her say it was still hurting her to another teacher while we were working on a science project on Tuesday morning. The next day she was gone, and Mr. Kilgore was to be our substitute teacher for the next two days.

We all arrived at school and waited in the gym until the first bell rang to go to class. We were greeted by Mr. Kilgore as we entered the room. Freda took the breakfast cart and brought it into the room and began handing the food to the students, as this was her week to do so. Of those who ate, she checked off the names from a roster that was clipped on a clipboard. After we all finished eating, Freda brought around the large trash bag for us to dump our trash and uneaten food into. She then put the cart, the roster, and the trash bag out in the hall. We were a little noisier than usual.

I heard Paul say to Roberto, "He doesn't know the rules. We're gonna have a blast for the next two days." They then high-fived each other. Shortly after that, Betty, Ruth, and Sista began talking and giggling. Soon, the whole class was talking, and Mr. Kilgore had to raise his voice to get us quiet. Mr. Kilgore told us to open our science books to page 254, but only about half the class did. This was going to be a rough two days.

Paul and Roberto got out of their seats and chased each other around the room. The next thing I remember was a very loud noise. It was Mr. Kilgore blowing a whistle. Every one stopped what they were doing. Yes, even Paul and Roberto stopped running and went to their seats. Something was about to change. Some saw it coming, but others didn't, and they would be the ones to suffer the consequences of their actions.

Mr. Kilgore made an announcement in a gentle yet firm voice. "I have a reward for those who have their book open to the correct page, a blank sheet of paper, a pencil, and your conduct card on the top of your desk." He then said, "You all have thirty seconds to comply with those instructions." Out of twenty-four students, six did not complete the task assigned.

"And ... five ... four ... three ... two ... one ... time is up," he said. Mr. Kilgore then walked around to each student's desk. He took the conduct cards and placed a checkmark in the column that read *Not following directions* on those six students' cards. Those six students were upset and said it wasn't fair. Mr. Kilgore continued walking around the room as if he didn't hear them.

Roberto turned to me and said, "It's not fair that *Mr. Old Guy* marked up my conduct card. Who does he think he is? Doesn't he know who I am? I got friends in low places that will take care of him. He's just some old has-been geezer."

"Yeah, I know what you mean," I said, with not much interest.

"Besides," Roberto continued, "I—"

"Please be quiet over there," interrupted Mr. Kilgore.

"Yes, sir, Mr. Kilgore," returned Roberto. "Hey, Blake, you don't think he heard me, do you?" he said softly.

"I'm not sure," I whispered.

"I can't afford to get into any more trouble—"

Mr. Kilgore then declared, "I have two rules that I strictly enforce. The first rule is to raise your hand and get permission to speak. The second rule is to not get out of your seat without *my* permission. Is that clear?"

All of the class responded with "Yes, Mr. Kilgore."

Although we all said we understood, there were a few that really didn't think he meant what he said. I'm here to tell you that Mr. Kilgore really did mean it. And you guessed it; it was the same six that had to spend time out in the hall before they learned he *really* meant it. Four of them finally learned.

Paul and Roberto never got it, and they were sent to the

office by a referral from Mr. Kilgore. This took place around nine o'clock, and they never came back to any of their remaining classes the rest of the day. While at lunch, some other kids said they passed by the In-School Suspension (ISS) room and saw them in there. I found out later that they had to complete the same classwork we did, plus some extra work.

The rest of the class settled down and got some serious learning accomplished and had an enjoyable time doing it. Mr. Kilgore was humorous and told some really funny science jokes and added some of his life experiences. That was our reward, and it made working on our science assignment a lot more enjoyable. I liked Mr. Kilgore.

Some Things to Think About

1. Have you ever met someone like Mr. Kilgore?

2. Would you like Mr. Kilgore as a substitute teacher?

3. What rules do you have in your home?

4. Name some rules you have in your classroom.

5. Name some rules you have in your city.

6. Name a rule you will have in your home when you grow up.

7. Tell why you would have that rule.

Fieldtrip

One rat said to the other rat,
"I smell cheese. Let's go get it!"
"Why?" said the other rat.
"It's what we do," replied the rat.

Ms. Bopart: "Thank you, students, for coming into first period so quietly. I'm back, and my tooth feels so much better. I'm pleased that Mr. Kilgore was able to fill in for me the past two days. I have some exciting news to report. As promised, we will be loading on the bus at about eight forty-five this morning for the big fieldtrip. Unfortunately, Paul and Roberto will not be with us, as they each got an extra day in ISS for not completing their assignment while there. Anyway, we only have a few minutes, so please finish your breakfast, as we can't dilly dally around."

Blake: "Wow, a fieldtrip. I bet we'll see some dinosaurs and a lion or two."

Buddy: "Yeah, and I bet a barracuda from the ocean!"

A Few Minutes Later

Ms. Bopart: "Please put away all of the items from your desktop and line up at the door for the field trip."

Blake: "After the trip, I'm going to write about it in my journal for an extra English class project grade."

Blake's Journal—Sixth-Grade English
My Fieldtrip
By Blake Sloan

I went on a fieldtrip, and the first thing I saw after getting off of the bus was a giant statue of a bird. The bird was a stork and must have been over a hundred feet tall. Our guide, Mr. Burns, said it was only ten feet tall. I told my friend, Buddy, that they should measure it again because it looked a lot taller than ten feet. All of my classmates agreed with me. Mr. Burns gathered us, and we entered the Lookout Exhibit Building.

Our teacher, Ms. Bopart, signed our group in on the sign-in roster just inside the door. Mr. Burns, our main guide, walked us down a hallway to see a room full of slithering snakes. My friend yelled out, "I've been bitten," but no one took him to the nurse.

He must have been kidding, as Ms. Bopart took him down the hall and talked to him. I saw him against the wall and not saying a word as Ms. Bopart pointed her finger at him, in his face, and neither of them was smiling. He returned and was very quiet, as he had to be at the back of the line for the rest of the tour.

Buddy, my best friend in that class, said one of the snakes was over fifty feet long. "I doubt it," I said. "Maybe fifty feet, but certainly not over fifty feet."

Buddy came back with, "Well, if he eats a big meal today and tomorrow, he'll be over fifty feet." Buddy had some good logic sometimes, and I couldn't disagree with him on that one.

Next, we entered a much larger room with a very high ceiling. The room must have been over a mile long and had a zillion stations. The first station had *beaucoup*—that means *a whole bunch of*—white mamma rabbits with a billion or so baby rabbits. I learned that word, *beaucoup*, from my Cajun friend, Justin, last summer. We got to pick up the rabbits and hold them, but we had to be seated on the floor before we could do that, as instructed by our guide. They were so very fluffy and white like snow. They reminded me of the rabbits that my brother, Bengy, was taking care of for his FFA project.

My rabbit was quiet and cuddly. Buddy's rabbit was all over the place and hard to hold. Twice, his rabbit jumped out of his grasp, and he had to pick him up again. After gently handling the baby rabbits, we returned them to Mr. Burns and his rabbit assistant, Ms. Amy. We were then led to the next station.

Bees. Cool. I didn't know that bees make honey. How could a little tiny bee make so much honey? I have a whole jar of honey at home. I now call it bee poop. Mom doesn't like me calling it that. I say, "Please pass the bee poop," and then she frowns at me. I also learned that when a bee finds a source of food, it flies back to the hive where the other bees live. The bee then dances in front of the other bees to tell them where to find the food. I wonder if they go to dance school interpretation to learn how to do that.

The next station was like a big lake. It had a million fish in it. All of the fish were different colors—some red, some orange, some blue, some white, and other colors too. Tall grass grew all along the edges of the water. The wall behind the water was painted blue with clouds all over. A walkway all the way around the water was cool to look from, and a bridge across the middle made it easy to look down into the water and see the fish.

The next station was a gigantic mesh cage with beaucoup birds flying around in it. The mesh cage was surrounded by another mesh cage, and that's where we stood and looked inside and saw birds—a lot of them. The chirping and squawking was loud. It was hard to hear Buddy when he talked to me. I just nodded my head as if I heard him, even though I didn't always understand what he said.

The forest woods station was awesome. It was a large, wooden, square building. I got on the step-up ladder and Mr. Poindexter, the guide for this section, handed me a flashlight. He lifted a tarp that covered a small, square hole in the side of the wall. I covered my head with the tarp and Mr. Poindexter told me to turn on the flashlight and look around the dark room. As I pointed the flashlight, I saw a tree that had a snake in it. I also saw another tree with an owl perched on a limb with shiny brown and yellow eyes.

Looking around some more, I saw a squirrel on the ground holding a pecan with his paws. Next I saw a raccoon that looked like it had a black mask over its eyes. Over in the back corner was a rabbit just sitting there. Shrubs and bushes covered most of the ground, and I saw some more birds in the trees. I asked Mr. Poindexter, "Why don't the animals move?" He said that they were stuffed. I guess that meant they ate too much. I don't like to move around very much when I'm stuffed either.

Well, our time was up, and we loaded back on the bus. I'll never forget the hundred-foot bird at the entrance, the fifty-foot snake, the billion rabbits, the bee poop, the million fish, and the animals that ate too much! I can hardly wait until April when we get to go again.

Some Things to Think About

1. Have you ever been to a place like this?

2. How many different colors of fish have you seen?

3. Would a really big snake scare you?

4. Would you let a snake crawl all over you?

5. What is your favorite animal in this story?

6. Have you ever climbed a tree?

7. Why can a cat climb a tree really fast?

It's Snow Time

Oh, the weather outside is frightening ... No! It's exciting!

Blake: "I woke up this morning to a pleasant surprise. I called all my buds and told them to look outside. They did, and they were ecstatic.

We arrived at school, and the Mackster said, "Look at all that snow on the ground! We're gonna have a good time in PE class today!"

"Oh, yes we are! Sweet times are waiting for us this afternoon!" exclaimed the Nose.

"Yep. I can hardly wait to show you guys how to throw a snowball and hit two people with it—you guys, that is," stated Slo-Mo.

"Hey, guys, the bell just rang, and we gotta get to class," Tex said.

In the Classroom

Ms. Bopart: "Come on in, students, and put your coats and backpacks up and then take a seat. We had some refreshing snow early this morning, and it's exciting, as we seldom see snow here in California. I know it's exciting, but we still have work to do. Get a drink of water, take one more look at the snow, and then be seated. Be sure you have paper and pencil, and don't forget to bring your brain with you to your seat as well.

"Let's get quiet, everyone. Please get out your science folders and put the map in front of you that I gave you yesterday.

"What? I can't believe that we have three students that can't find their map. You have got to be more responsible. All right, here you are. Everyone should have a map now. To help us get started, I would like us to sing a song to assist in welcoming our first snow, and most likely our only snow of the season. The words are on the board. Everyone look this way please. Is everyone ready to sing? Let's begin."

Yes, it's a great day here at Grape Field.
The grass has given way to snow.
The green has now come undone.
It's time for Grape Field fun ... we know!

The streets are wet, I tell you.
You better be careful and drive slow.
If you don't, you might end up blue.
And that might cost you some dough.

Later that Day—Just before Lunch

Ms. Bateman: "Joey, it's almost time for lunch. Will you take the lunch packet to Ms. Spooner in the cafeteria, please?"

Joey: "Yes, ma'am."

Ms. Bateman: "Thank you, Joey, and don't you dare lose them on the way there."

Joey: "I won't, Ms. Bateman. You can count on me!"

Five Minutes Later

Ms. Bateman: "Thank you, Joey. Did you get them there okay?"

Joey: "Yes, ma'am, I did."

A Few Seconds Later

Joey: "Psssst! Hey ... Andy. Hey ... Blake. You're not going to believe this."

Blake: "What is it?"

Andy: "Yeah, Joey, what gives?"

Joey: "There's almost no snow on the ground anymore!"

Blake and Andy together: "Say what!"

Andy: "You better not be lying or I'll deck you ... friend or not."

Joey: "I promise. I saw it through the window as I went to the cafeteria and again on the way back."

Ms. Bateman: "Attention class. Clear off your desks and line up and prepare to go to lunch ... this row line up first ... now this row ..."

"Attention class ... quiet over there and listen! Before we go to lunch I have an announcement. As you have noticed, the snow has melted and just about all gone, except in the shaded areas. I also know many of you were very much looking forward to playing in it in P. E. class.

Since that's not going to happen, I'd like to let you in on some information that I just found out. After lunch, and if you all are well behaved, *we* have a surprise waiting for you. No, don't ask me what it is as you will find out soon enough. Okay line leader, go ahead and lead the class to the cafeteria and enjoy your lunch ... and wait for the surprise!"

Students Entering the Lunch Room

Andy: "I bet the surprise is just to keep us from complaining."

Joey: "Yeah, I'm not buying into it."

Blake: "I bet it's something that's real stupid that only the nerds will like."

Kate: "Hey, you guys, why don't you knock it off and just wait and see what the surprise is."

Joey: "Hey, maybe it's gonna be a mud ball fight on the playground."

Andy: "Yeah, that would be the coolest."

Blake: "Maybe we'll throw one or two at Kate."

Kate: "You're all wrong. I know what it is."

Andy, Blake, and Joey (together): "What is it?"

Andy: "She doesn't know!"

Kate: "I do too! But I'm not telling."

Blake: "She doesn't know, I tell ya."

Kate: "Oh, yes I do. But I'm still not telling."

Ms. Bateman: "Sixth-graders, let me have your attention. As you know, the playground is too muddy to play on today. First and second periods had their PE this morning and got to play in the snow before it melted. Therefore, Principal Jensen has an announcement to make."

Principal Jenson: "Thank you, Ms. Bateman. I see most of you have completed your lunch, so ... students, are you ready for a treat?"

Cafeteria Students: "Yes, Mr. Jensen!"

Principal Jensen: "All righty then. We have for your eating pleasure snow cones with the school colors; half are in blueberry juice, and the other half of the snow cone is covered in pineapple gold juice. I hope you enjoy! And one more announcement: don't forget that next week is Fire Prevention Week all week long. Now please, enjoy your snow cones."

Kate: "Pretty cool, huh?"

Joey: "Yeah, it's okay."

Blake: "Hey, look at what Mr. Jensen and Ms. Bateman are doing. They're rolling out a big machine."

Andy: "It has some writing on it. What does it say?"

Kate: "Yeah, Blake, you better read it since Andy doesn't know how!"

Andy: "Shut up!"

Joey: "It says *snow-making machine.*"

Kate: "Look. It's blowing out snow, or at least it looks like snow."

Joey, Jim, Andy, and Kate (together): "This is the coolest!"

Some Things to Think About

1. Would you have been surprised like these students were?

2. Tell about a surprise that's happened to you.

3. What is the most fun thing to do in the snow?

4. Does it snow a lot where you live?

5. Have you ever slid down a snow hill?

Is that Really a Six-Foot Dog?

Fires are really awesome when they're needed to cook food.

My mom reminded me to get up early today because we need to pick up Ann and take her to school. Mom said something about Ann's parents and an out-of-town business trip. That's okay by me. Ann is pretty cute; yes, she's pretty *and* she's cute. I think she likes me too.

"Bengy, get out of the bathroom," I ordered. "I'm in a hurry!"

"What's a matter for you? You gotta hot date with Ann?" Bengy muttered.

"Maybe … maybe I do, and maybe I don't. Stick around bonehead, and it's just possible you might pick up some girl pick-up pointers from me," I retorted.

"Gee, you really think so? I don't," he retaliated.

"Right, I don't think so either. You're too dumb to learn them," I added while peering at him.

"No! You're the dumb one. I meant you don't have anything to teach … oh, never mind. Just for that, I'm gonna stay in here for a long, long time," Bengy stammered back.

"That's about how long it will take to wash the dirt out of *one* of your ears," I barked back.

"What's that you say?" said Bengy with laughter. "I can't hear you."

"You're pathetic," I said as I walked away to meet up with Ann.

"Ah, it was nice to see Ann," I whispered to myself after I greeted her.

"Don't forget this is Friday, the last day of Fire Prevention Week," Ann reminded me as she graciously entered the car.

"Yes, I know. It's been a fun week so far," I said.

"I wrote an English paper on this week's activities that I have to present today. Would you like to hear it? It will give me practice one last time," she said.

How could I say no? So I blurted out, "Sure."

As she gathered the papers from her notebook, she said, "Okay, it goes like this:

"My name is Ann, and this week is *Fire Prevention Week* at my school. Today is Friday, and our teacher, Ms. McKnight, is having the class write about some of our activities that happened for this special week. I have three things that happened that I would like to write about. The first thing that I will write about happened on Monday.

"My mom dropped me off in front of school like she always does. I had forgotten that this was Fire Prevention Week until I stepped out of the car. I waved good-bye to my mom as I walked up to the front of the school. I reached out to open the door decorated with red paper when a big dog, and I mean a *really big dog*, opened the door for me. At first I was a little frightened, but the dog shook my hand and said, 'Hello.'

"The dog was white with a whole lot of black spots on him. He was really tall too! He handed me and some other students a handout and a pamphlet. He then reminded us that this was Fire Prevention Week and wished us to have a great *fire-free day*. Then the dog said he would see us later in the week, and he departed, saying, 'Catch you later, gators.' After that, he went to greet other students with the same message. The next really cool thing that happened was on Tuesday.

"We marched down the hall in our straight lines to the cafeteria for lunch. The cafeteria ladies who gave us our lunch trays and food were dressed up. They really weren't dressed up, but their faces were painted like clowns. After we got our food, we punched our lunch number into the keypad. The lunch lady placed a little toy fire engine truck on our tray. After I sat down to eat my lunch, I noticed that our large oatmeal cookie was shaped like a firefighter. The lunchroom teachers that come around and help the kindergarten and first-graders open their milk cartons or tear open the ketchup packets for them were painted with clown faces too. The best painted face was Ms. Pepper. She had a big, red nose, red pigtails, really thick, black-framed glasses, and blackish and brown dotted freckles on her face. That was the best lunchtime ever!

"On Thursday, we were all called to go to the gymnasium for a presentation. We were really packed together as we sat on the floor of the gym. Our principal stepped up to the microphone and got everyone quiet. She then introduced the *Fire Team Leader*, Mr. Knothead.

"Mr. Knothead had on a very nice suit with a tie, but he had a clown's face. He had two assistants, dressed as clowns, who were being recruited and trained to be on the fire team. It was Mr. Knothead's task to train them, with our help.

"The recruits weren't very knowledgeable since *we*, the audience, had to give the answers that they couldn't get. A dog puppet in the background would hold up the answers for us to say when asked a question. It was a lot of fun, and we all laughed really hard and a lot. We had fun and learned lots of information about fire safety. I will end this paper with some things we learned and by saying I really enjoyed this *Fire Prevention Week*!" Then she read her list of things she learned.

Some Things We Learned

1. If your clothes catch on fire, you need to: stop, drop, roll, and cover your face.

2. Have a plan to escape (door, window, and places like those) in case your home catches on fire.

3. Practice the plan as a family.

4. Get a rope ladder for upstairs if you live in a home with an upstairs.

5. Don't play around with matches or a lighter. If someone is playing with these, tell an adult, such as a teacher or your parents or some other responsible adult.

Some Things to Think About

1. Have you attended a fire-safety presentation at your school? If so, tell about your fire-safety presentation. Was it as fun as Ann's?

2. Describe the funniest clown you have ever seen.

3. Describe how the clown was dressed. Did the clown have on a tie? Did the clown have big shoes?

4. Was the clown a man or a woman?

Shy Girl

Hey, look at that girl over there.
Is she shy or just really smart?

Today is a special day. About six weeks ago, I signed up for a project to assist an elementary teacher at one of the elementary schools in our district ... all day. I was selected and notified last week so I could be prepared for today. I was given a packet of papers that would help prepare me for the task. I'm here to tell you, that packet didn't prepare me for what I was about to experience!

I arrived on time like the packet instructed me to. I was doing fine so far, so I gave myself two thumbs-up for that. I assisted the teacher by helping distribute breakfast to the students. I got to eat too. After that, we began math time. I passed out the math assignment to the fourth-graders. I don't remember being as small as these fourth-graders were. It must be the food they feed them nowadays.

About ten minutes into the math work, and after assisting some of them with the math, I found myself with nothing to do. I took a place in the back of the class and waited. And then I heard an interesting conversation between two girls. The conversation went like this:

Conversation #1

"Hello, Sandy. I'm glad to see you. We're in the fourth grade this year, and I'm so excited! Soon we'll be graduating from high school and getting married and get jobs. Wow! So, what do you want to be when you grow up?"

"I want to be a piano player. No! I meant to say, I want to play the piano. There's a difference you know. I've been practicing since the first grade, and now I'm older and more mature. I just cannot wait to get to the sixth grade where I'll finally be out of elementary school and not around these children, or more like babies, that go here.

"I'm not talking about you, because you're more like me, mature. I ... I mean *we* are ready for the nicer things that middle school has to offer. I have an older sister that goes to Grape Field Middle School already, and I can hardly wait to go there too! I mean, do *you* want to be around some of the *children* we're around any longer than you *have* to be?

"Just between you and me, Jimmy is a copycat and makes fun of me all the time. Let me tell you, just last week I was in line, and he let my friend Kathy cut in front of the lunch line, but he wouldn't let *me*. I had to watch them eat while I was still waiting in line to get my food.

"But I have an idea. Come closer, and I'll tell you about my plan, but you have to promise not to tell anyone. The next time he tries to copy my science work, well, he's in for a big surprise. I'm going to put down the wrong answers and pretend I'm not looking and let him copy all he wants. After he does and he's finished, I'm going to erase the wrong answers and put in the correct ones. I'll show him! I know how to get even as well as get ahead."

"Shhhh … he might hear us."

Some Things to Think About

1. How does it make you feel when someone copies your work?

2. How do you handle someone cheating with work you've done?

3. Is there a better way Sandy could have handled the situation she was in?

4. What are some ways you have handled a similar situation?

5. Do you ever wish you could be older?

6. If you could be older, what age would you want to be? Why that age?

Restroom Mix-Up

Pay no attention to the girl behind the door;
she always screams when in the restroom!

My duties continued as I assisted Ms. Mumford in preparing the students for recess. Restroom break was first, and then recess would follow. Most of the students had exited the building and were racing to the playground. I was asked to stay inside and monitor those who needed a *potty* break while Ms. Mumford would be just on the other side of the glass door to monitor the students playing outside. While the students were waiting their turn for the restroom (one at a time) in their respective boy and girl lines, I heard another interesting conversation.

Conversation #2

"Oh, Carol, I'm glad it's recess, and it's time for jump rope. Only a few more minutes, and I'm going to be jumping rope and showing Nicole, Linda, and Beth that I'm the best jump rope girl at Grape Grove Elementary School. But first I gotta pee really, really bad."

"Okay fourth-graders," I interjected, "let's keep the lines straight for the bathroom break and get ready for recess time. And please hurry! You're wasting your recess time."

"Oh, I can't wait to show the girls my new jump rope song. It goes like this: *Cinderella dressed in yella, went upstairs to kiss a fella. And by mistake, she kissed a snake. How many doctors did it take? One ... two ... three ... four ... five ... six ... seven ...*"

"Let's keep the line moving. Recess time is waiting for you," I reminded.

"Hey, Jo-Jo, it's your turn," said Carol.

"I'm going, and don't rush me."

The door to the bathroom closed.

A minute later, I heard a scream and asked, "Is everything okay in there?"

"Er, uh, yes Mr. Blake," said Jo-Jo.

"Wow—*Mr. Blake*," I said to myself. I think that was the first time I'd ever been called Mr. before. And although I don't think

I was meant to hear, I barely heard what came next from behind the restroom door.

"Oh man, I can't believe I got water all down my front while washing my hands. I can't let the jump rope girls see *me like this*. They'll make fun of me and spread rumors that I peed on myself. What am I going to do?"

Some Things to Think About

1. Here are some ideas that Jo-Jo thought of while she was in the restroom:

   - Tie her sweater around her waist so it will hide the water on her clothes.
   - Use the hand blow dryer to dry her clothes.
   - Open the door, step outside, and don't worry about it.
   - Cry until the clothes dry.
   - Splash more water over different parts of her clothes so it will look more like an accident, one the jump rope girls wouldn't make fun of.

   Which was her best idea?

2. How would you handle this situation?

Friends

Friends are special people that you can share things with.

What have I gotten myself into? The great adventure didn't end there. I finally got Jo-Jo taken care of and the rest of the students out to the playground. Ms. Mumford then asked me to keep an eye on the girls that were close to the building while she moved closer to the playground area. Soon, the girls forgot I was standing a little ways behind them and began talking.

Conversation #3

Breanna: "I love my long, dark hair. I feel beautiful when I comb it every morning and at night before I go to bed. See these new combs my mom bought me for Christmas? They're ivory white with swirls of black. The combs glide through my hair easily because it's so silky smooth."

Shaunee: "You do have beautiful hair, and it's nice to touch. Look at this! My mom let me take this pinkish lipstick to school today, but don't tell her 'cause she already knows. Help me put some on. Doesn't it look pretty on my lips?"

Chanette: "Yes, it makes you look older and more grown up. But hey, how about this? Do you like my new earrings? See what happens when I shake my head?"

Breanna: "Oh, wow, they glow and sparkle! You're so lucky to have those sparkly earrings. I want a pair like them."

Chanette: "You can't buy them anymore because I bought the last pair. I don't think they make them anymore. I think they only made just this one set. I'm lucky I got them when I did."

Shaunee: "You *are* lucky! Look here and see how lucky I am too."

Breanna: "Oh my goodness! You are lucky! Where did you get those? I just want to know. Where, oh where?"

Shaunee: "I won them in a drawing at that big new jewelry store in the mall."

Chanette: "Oh, oh, oh, they're beautiful. I want some too!"

Blake: "Breanna, Shaunee, Chanette. Don't you girls want to play and run around? Recess is almost over."

Girls Together: "No, we like what we're doing."

Breanna: "Besides, Mr. Blake, we *are* playing and having fun."

Blake: "Okay, but not much longer because in a few minutes we need to go inside and get ready for the math quiz." *Oh, good grief! I'm not sure what I want to be when I grow up, but it's not a teacher!*

Some Things to Think About

1. What do you think Shaunee had that the other girls liked so much?

2. Tell about something you have that you really like.

3. Tell about something you *don't* have that you would really like to have.

4. Do you have a good friend that you share things with?

5. Who is your best friend?

6. Tell a partner about something you did with a friend.

Class Leader

Follow me and see where it gets you.

After my responsibilities as assistant to the teacher were completed at the end of the day, I pondered this experience. What an eye opener this had been! The packet requested me to write a summary of my day, which I did. It further stated that I had to write a paper about leadership qualities I observed, which I also accomplished. Then the hard part came. I had to write about a student in my life that exemplified leadership. Without hesitation, I recalled Alvin from a year back.

This was going to be easier than I thought. I began to write about Alvin.

Alvin was his name, and he was our class leader. He wasn't elected or anything like that; he was just a very likeable person. He got to do things for the teacher because she liked him too. If she needed something taken to the office or to the school nurse, it was Alvin that was chosen to take it most of the time. He wasn't snobby about it either; it was just a job to do, according to him. It made him big in our eyes, and so we would on occasion call him Big Al.

When out on the playground and other kids began to argue, it was Alvin that they would go to for settling their differences. His decisions were considered and usually accepted and obeyed. He was always fair and considerate of both sides and made his decisions so both sides came out winners. This ensured that he came out a winner too, and he did.

Alvin never missed school, and I can't think of a time when he was sick or even went to the school nurse. When it came to classwork, he never had to say, "Can I turn this in late or at another time?" He was on task and always on the ball. "How come we have to do this" never came out of his mouth.

After a while, when we would be reading a book at reading time, some would say, "What page are we on?" But it didn't come from Alvin, as he knew what page, paragraph, and sentence we were on and would be the first to assist those who were lost. He was helpful like that.

When we were in writing time, there would be those that asked, "Is this for a grade?" or they might say, "How long does this have to be?" even after the teacher had already told the class those things. But it was never Alvin; he knew to do his best, and he did. He listened and followed instructions from the teacher, the first time and every time.

At the end of fifth grade last year, our principal, Ms. Hillard, made a special announcement. She stated that this fifth-grade class was the best she had graduated to the Middle High School level in her fourteen years of being the principal at Grape Grove Elementary. She also said our test scores said the same thing, and she continued by saying that we were well prepared for the sixth grade!

After Ms. Hillard said all of that, each of us looked at each other with big smiles and a sense of achievement. I couldn't help but notice that each student in that class at one time or another looked in Alvin's direction with a knowing look of appreciation. Yes, we all knew it was Alvin's example that inspired us to do our best, as he did his best.

Alvin didn't go on to the sixth grade with us, as he moved off to Montana somewhere.

I closed the paper with:

Thanks, Alvin, wherever you are.

Some Things to Think About

1. Do you know someone like Alvin?

2. How much are you like Alvin?

3. No one said Alvin was the smartest in the class, but do you think he made good grades?

4. "Always try and always do your best." Is that a good motto to follow?

5. What do you want to get better at in your class?

6. What are you good at that you can help others with?

Visit to the Mackster's Grandparents

A step back in time to a grand place!

"Hello. Is the Mackster there? ... May I speak with him, please? ...

"Hey, Mackster. This is Blake, and you were right. Your grandfather's house is the best! I was just over there last night visiting with my mom. She brought over a freshly baked pie for your grandparents. I saw all the things you've been telling me about at school the past couple of months. I do hope your grandpa gets over his bad cold. Maybe the pie we brought over will help.

"When we stepped into the entranceway, I saw the wagon wheel and saddle lamp sitting on the narrow, long table against the wall. It had two cactus plants on each side and a metal tree with dangly things on it. Some of the dangly things were spurs, boots, saddles, horseshoes, horses, and cactus plants. It was cool, just like you told me.

"Above that display was a picture of your grandparents, but they were all dressed up in old Western clothes, and your grandpa had a rifle across his lap. Your grandma was dressed in a really nice, long, blue dress with a big hat with shaggy things hanging all the way around the brim."

"Did you see the wall with all the cars?" the Mackster asked.

"Yes," I responded. "I turned the corner, and there the wall was, just like you said. I saw the wall with all the classic muscle cars from the 1950s and 1960s. I saw the Pontiac GTO. There were a couple of Chevelle Super Sport vehicles, also a couple of Corvettes, a very classic 1957 Chevy, and I saw a Dodge Charger, as well as many other cool cars. It was great."

"Did you get to go upstairs? That's the best," said the Mackster.

"Well," I continued, "as I looked up the stairs, I noticed the stair landing. It had a nice stereo, and on each side was a free-standing lifelike picture—of Elvis Presley on the left, and Marilyn Monroe on the right. Centered between them on the wall was a metal sign that read: Rock & Roll. On each side of the sign were two guitars; one was blue, and the other red. Above the stereo but underneath the metal sign was an album with a picture cover of the famous rock and roll band known as the Beatles. Your grandma then said something to me. She asked if I would like to go upstairs and see the movie room. 'Awesome,' was all I could say.

"And awesome the room is. The movie room has an eighty-two-inch television with a surround sound system. Around the room, I noticed lots of pictures. I saw a poster from the movie *American Graffiti*, various signs that read: Popcorn, Movie Night, Lights, Camera, and Action. On one wall was a bullhorn that a director uses to direct movies. A large poster had all the *Star Wars* characters in it, and there was another poster that had all the Marvel Comic characters in it.

"Another shelf had an Oscar award mounted on it and a VIP (Very Important Person) Entrance sign above that. I did feel important, I should say! I also noticed that the windows were covered with dark blue curtains, and over one of the windows hung a sign that read: Hollywood Walk of Fame. It had long, silver streamers all the way to the floor. In front of the television were six movie chairs that had cup holders on each side. Then I saw the coolest thing, but I'll tell you about that tomorrow at school, as you don't know about it since they just recently got it.

"Then your grandma asked about you and about school, and I said we were best friends, and she said she knew that. Then she asked if I'd like to come over sometime with you and watch a movie, and I said yes. So, Mackster, when would you like to go over so I can call her back with a time and a date?"

"It sounds like it would be fun, and maybe we can ask her if the Nose, Slo-Mo, and Tex can come too," the Mackster responded.

"Yeah. Now *that* sounds like an adventure!"

Some Things to Think About

1. Describe the coolest house you've ever seen.

2. Is the coolest house you've seen yours or someone else's?

3. What do you think Blake saw that he wouldn't tell the Mackster about until later (at the end of the story)?

4. What is your favorite movie or television show?

5. Does your family ever have a movie night? If so, what do you do during your family movie night?

My Name Is <u>Not</u> Dennis

When was the last time you tried to do something right, but you were misunderstood?

"Hi, guys. Man, am I glad to see you four. I just almost got beaten up by some eighth-graders."

"What happened to you, Blake ole boy?" said Tex.

"Well, I was running a bit late to school this morning, and I decided to go in from the side entrance. Little known to me, that's where the eighth-graders hang out," I explained.

"I could have told you that," said the Mackster.

"Well, I wish you had … before today," I returned. "There I was at a fast walk and minding my own business, when three of the biggest guys I've ever seen on this campus stepped in front of me. They asked me what grade I was in, and I told them that I was a sixth-grader and that I was almost late and I needed to get to class. Then one of them got real close to me and said, 'Hey, little bitty, teeny weenie sixth-grader, you picked the wrong door to come in. This here door is for eighth-graders *only*.'"

"You should have told them you were a new student," said the Nose.

"Yeah, that's what I would have told them," said Slo-Mo.

"Well, I didn't think about that. I wish I had," I retorted. "Anyway, after all the pushing, they made me go around. The worst thing was that there were several eighth-grade girls standing by giggling their heads off the whole time."

"Wow, you're lucky to be standing here alive with us now," said Tex.

"Yes, but I got 'em back. As I was leaving, and a good safe distance away, I shouted, 'Do you know what they call a good-looking eighth-grade girl on this campus?'

"'What?' they said.

"'A visitor!' I yelled. And then I scampered out of there. Real fast."

"Good job and way to go," my buds said as they high-fived me.

"Hey, we got to get to class. Besides, Dennis, or whatever his name is, was absent when we gave our reports a few weeks ago, and today he's giving his make-up report in English class. It's supposed to be good. We'll see. He said the report is about that skit he was in a couple of years ago."

"I remember that skit," said the Nose. "Well, see you later, gator."

English Class Later that Day

"Okay, class," announced Ms. Simpson, "Daryl was absent when you all presented you're reports, and today is the make-up day for that. Go ahead, Daryl, and please watch your step. It seems the entire class has had a bad case of *stumble-itis* when giving their reports."

Daryl did stumble and made this apologetic statement to the class and Ms. Simpson in particular: "Sorry, I guess I've made it a 100 percent thing on the stumbling."

The class burst out in laughter, and Ms. Simpson said, "Class, settle down. Go ahead, Daryl."

And then Daryl began.

"They call me the Menace, but my name is not Dennis. It is Daryl. I don't see myself as destructive, as I'm mostly helpful. How I got the nickname is more from my bumbling ways than from ill manners or bad intentions. I have a story that explains how it all came about.

"Two years ago, my elementary school sponsored a variety show to be presented to the whole school, and this was to take place during our assembly hour. Each presentation was to be limited to two minutes, no longer. We would be allowed to do a single presentation, work with a partner, or work in a group that could not exceed five students. I was in a group of four presenters, and we chose to do a skit. A total of twenty-one skits would be presented, and our group was to be number twelve in the order.

"Our group practiced for several weeks, and the big day finally came. Each of us arrived to school early and gathered at the front door, as we had agreed to. We then took our props and costumes to the cafeteria stage where Ms. Miller and Ms. Jones were waiting to assist us with storing them until the show began. As our group walked out of the cafeteria, we were high-fiving each other and shouting that we were number one and we were are going to win!

"We continued to class, and toward the later part of first period, we were called out to prepare for our presentation. About halfway through second period, the rest of the students filed into the cafeteria area, which now was an auditorium filled with students, teachers, and some parents. It was noisy at first until Ms. Miller stepped up to the microphone and got everyone quiet. After the audience was quieted down, Ms. Miller began her introduction, and the program was under way.

"The first presentation went well and set the tone for the show. Backstage, between the presentations, it got noisy with everyone running around. There were those departing the stage and throwing off their costumes, and then there were those going onto the stage and trying to make their last-minute adjustments to *their* costumes. It was hectic, as costumes and props got mixed up, which got Ms. Jones involved. It caused a few arguments among some of the kids, but thankfully she got things sorted out, settled everyone down, and got things back to normal. Like she would always say, 'The show must go on!'

"Our turn! We were next to present. This was exciting and scary at the same time. The first minute of the skit went well, just as we had planned ... and then it happened. I was to come running out on the stage dressed in a green costume with an ugly face mask. Then I was to jump up and down and scare the audience. At that point, we had four girls in the front row who, on cue, were to start running and screaming down the aisles, between some of the rows of chairs, and among the audience. This final scene was to end our skit.

"I came running out all right, and I was right on cue, just as rehearsed. While I stood staring at the audience, I was waiting for the girls to start running ... but they didn't. *What went wrong?* I wondered. Something was wrong, but I didn't know what. Janet finally stepped over by me and pointed at my head and face and shouted, 'Oh, no, it's the Menace of Hillsboro Hills! See how ugly he is!' As she pointed at me, I only then realized that I had forgotten my mask and that my face was not covered.

"The audience began snickering, kids were rolling on the floor laughing, and the girls were *still* not running. A boy from the right side of the audience jumped up from his chair and shouted while pointing at me, 'It's the ugly menace!' This created another roar of laughter while I just stood there. Finally, the girls began running.

"We didn't win first place, but we did get *honorable mention*, which translates to fourth place. Although we didn't win, our skit was talked about the rest of the year and after, and the first, second, and third places were soon forgotten.

"And that, my fellow classmates, is how I got the nickname of the Menace ... but my name is *not* Dennis."

"Way to go, Dennis ... I mean Daryl," I stated as he left the front of the class.

"Thanks, Blake," said Daryl as he sat down. "I'm glad that's over."

"I know what you mean," I responded.

Some Things to Think About

1. Do you have a nickname? If so, what is your nickname and how did you get it?

2. Have you ever been in a play or skit?

3. Tell about a skit you were in or one you saw.

4. Have you ever made a mistake in front of your friends? How did you feel? Did anyone help you feel better about your mistake?

Bikes and the Race

Do you like to race? I'll race you!

"On your mark, get set, go!"

The race was on. My bike was the fastest thing on two wheels in the whole neighborhood. I hadn't been beaten in about a year. But that didn't keep the competition away, and I had to keep putting them down as they came to challenge me, which allowed my reputation to build even higher. The race was to the local

Dairy Queen about six and a half blocks from my house. I have a theory on why I win so much.

I think if the others knew how much I like ice cream, they would know my secret. I *love* ice cream! The other guys like it, but I *love* it! I like it, I love it, I want some more of it! I just can't get enough of it! That's my motto. As I said, I haven't been beat in a bike race in about a year. Ummmm, that's just about how long ago the DQ came into this neighborhood. I wonder if there's a connection. Well, anyway, I came to a sliding, screeching halt as I locked my brakes in front of the DQ entrance.

"First again!" I yelled as I laid my bike down. I then did my championship dance around it with my finger pointing into the air while chanting, "I'm number one! I'm number one!" Then came the Mackster, and then the Nose, and then Tex, and yes ... Slo-Mo. Another thing I like about being first is that last place has to buy the ice cream for first place—just another little incentive to be first.

"Hey, what are we waiting for? Let's get some ice cream," said Slo-Mo.

"Good thinking," clamored the Mackster.

"Last one in is a rotten egg," declared Tex.

We shoved ourselves through the door all at once. With all the squirming and pushing, we would have gotten to the counter to order sooner if we had gone through one at a time. But to five wanna-be winners, that would not have made sense, and it would not have been nearly as much fun.

"May I help you, boys?" said the counter lady.

"Yes, Ms. Wanda, you certainly may," Slo-Mo blurted but in a respectful manner.

"I'm glad to see you boys again on another pleasant, sunny Saturday afternoon," Ms. Wanda cordially said. "Who won the race today?"

"I did," we all enthusiastically said.

"Wow, so it was a five-way tie?" she asked.

"Technically, my nose got here first, but the rules say the bike and rider must completely arrive at the same time, so that ruled me out … or maybe I won by a nose!" said the Nose.

"I would have been first, but I got a slow … no, they all started before I said go," said Slo-Mo.

"I *do* think that Blake's bike had his wheel over the start line," declared the Mackster.

I shook my head.

"Come on, Snake, you know it's true," said Tex.

"Maybe, maybe not. You got the video in your pocket to prove it?" I retorted.

"So, Blake won, I am to assume," said Ms. Wanda. "What about you, Tex? What do you say?"

"I say I want to order a chocolate sundae with lots of nuts," Tex proudly said.

"I want the same," we all chimed in.

"Put more nuts on mine than on anyone else's," demanded the Nose.

"He needs it to stay nutty," the Mackster said.

"Okay, I got four—no—five chocolate sundaes," said Ms. Wanda.

"That's right," we sang back.

"Five sundaes on a Saturday," Ms. Wanda said. "Have a seat, and I'll have them right out."

"That booth … last one there is a butthead," the Mackster said as he pointed toward the booth.

Napkins laid out, spoons in hand, eyes as big as half dollars, and here came Ms. Wanda with the anticipated sundaes. Nothing but elbows and mouths could be seen for the next five minutes.

There was an occasional brain freeze, but other than that, there was nothing but paradise in that booth among us five.

"I can't think of anything that beats this," said Slo-Mo as he finished his sundae with a loud burp.

"I can't—" I stopped in midsentence.

As I looked up, I noticed a girl standing next to our booth. She was looking at all of us rather disgustingly.

"You naughty boys," she said in a sophisticated way. "I heard about your texting some girls in the cafeteria the other day. You should be ashamed of yourselves."

"Hi, Rose. How are you?" I asked. "And what are you talking about?"

Slo-Mo let out another belch that was louder than the first one.

"Don't you know you shouldn't do that in front of a girl?" Rose said.

"Sorry, he didn't know it was your turn. He'll wait for you to burp first next time," said the Nose.

"You boys are something else," Rose declared.

I could discern that Rose approached us for a different reason than the one she was leading us to believe. It wasn't our *disgusting* behavior ... it was something else. I then asked Rose, "Would you like a bite of my sundae?"

Rose pleasantly replied, "I'm with some friends, and we've already placed our order."

"Would you like to sit with us?" Tex said.

"Not today. Besides, you're almost through, we're just getting started, and it would be crowded," Rose replied. "Maybe some other time. See ya."

As Rose was walking away, she turned, and while looking me straight in the eyes, she said with only her mouth moving and no voice, "Text me sometime."

"Hey, guys, we need to get going," Tex said. "My parents are supposed to pick me up at three o'clock, and it's getting close to that now."

"Okay, but one last thing," said Slo-Mo. *Burrrrrp!*

"Thanks," said the Mackster sarcastically.

"I needed that—not," said Tex.

"Not," said the Nose.

"Don't forget, next weekend is movie night at the Mackster's grandparents'," I said. Then I squeezed in a gangster pose and added, "See ya later!"

"Not if I see you first," the Nose slyly answered.

"Thanks for the warning," said the Mackster.

Some Things to Think About

1. Do you have a favorite place to hang out?

2. What do you think about ice-cream sundaes?

3. What would you have ordered?

4. What toppings on your ice cream would you request?

5. Would you text Rose if she asked you to?

6. Have you ever raced on your bike?

7. When you go to a restaurant, do you prefer a booth or a table? Why?

Movie Night

Please pass the popcorn! Shhhhh ...
I'm trying to watch the movie.

"Welcome, boys," said Mr. Mack as he greeted us at the door. "Maw Mack is preparing the popcorn," he continued. "We're gonna have a rootin', shootin', tootin' good time tonight. I've got the movie you boys wanted and another one if that one isn't enough."

"What?" questioned Maw Mack. "Do you think these boys can keep their eyes open long enough for two back-to-back movies? I'm sure they will need to be put to bed before that."

"Nonsense and hogwash," defended Paw Mack. "They can stay up for a *third* movie if they want to. We just might watch it with them."

"Maybe you, but not me," Maw Mack said with finality.

"Hey, is that popcorn ready? I can hear these boys' stomachs growling from here for it, Maw Slowpoke," said Paw Mack.

"It's almost ready, Paw Grouchy," Maw Mack returned. "Why don't you show the boys your new toy, and then it should be ready."

"Oh yeah, come on, boys. Come out here to the screened-in porch and see what I recently got," Paw Mack announced.

"Is it what I saw the last time I was here?" I inquired.

"Sure enough is, Blake," said Paw Mack.

"I told you your Paw got something new, and now you're getting ready to see it," I said to the Mackster.

"I can't wait," the Mackster said.

"Wow, a pool table!" exclaimed the Nose.

"That's cool," added Tex

"Super," chimed in Slo-Mo.

"Here's the popcorn, and the sodas are iced down in a tub on the kitchen table," Maw Mack announced. "Maybe you boys can beat Paw in a game of pool before you start your movies."

After a few miscues and a ball or two hopping over a rail and rolling onto the floor, we were finally getting the hang of the game. But after our second game ended, Slo-Mo knocked over a lamp with his cue stick. We knew it was time to go start the movie when Paw Mack suggested we do so.

"Grab another soda and more popcorn before going to the movie room," said Maw Mack.

"Are you sure these boys ought to be watching this movie?" said Maw Mack in a teasing yet mildly protesting voice.

"What, this movie—*Dumb and Dumber*? Of course. It's very funny," said Paw Mack in our defense. "And this one is in 3-D," he added.

Turning to us, Paw Mack instructed, "You boys take a seat in the movie chairs and put your sodas in the cup holders on either side of the chair when you're not drinking them. And oh yes, try not to get popcorn on the floor, as I recommend the best place for the popcorn is in your mouth. It tastes better that way. Okay, settle down and try not to smack your popcorn in your mouth too loud, as the movie is about to start. Lights … camera … and … action! Also, don't forget your 3-D glasses."

Although we had seen this movie before, but not in 3-D, we laughed ourselves silly *again*. Sitting behind us were Paw and Maw Mack. Maw Mack was also knitting, and then she said to Paw Mack, "Are you sure they should be watching this?" Paw Mack didn't answer but kept on laughing.

Shortly after that, I heard Slo-Mo say, "Here comes the bathroom scene, my favorite part."

Sure enough, for five guys, it was as funny this time as it was the first time … maybe funnier! I guess that's what happens when people laugh together; it keeps the laughter going and going. I was laughing *so* very hard; we all were.

"Stop, I can't take anymore," pleaded the Nose as he rolled out of his chair and onto the floor with laughter.

Although still in my chair, I was holding my sides as the laughter continued. The Mackster, Slo-Mo, and Tex looked like a bunch of monkeys as they thrashed around in their chairs with their laughing. I looked backward and, out of the corner of my eye, I got a glimpse of Maw Mack as she slapped her knee and then wiped tears from her eyes with both of her hands from her laughter. Maw Mack didn't say anything more about us not watching the movie; she was too busy laughing. She even stopped knitting and put it aside throughout the remainder of the movie.

A little later, I got a tingling feeling in my thigh. I thought maybe I had laughed so hard that I might have pulled a muscle. It went away, but only to come back a few seconds later and again a third time. I finally realized it was my cell phone, which I had on vibrate. I fumbled it out of my pocket and saw that I had a text message. The text read:

It's late. Spending the night at Carla's and Jennifer's house ... call me tomorrow after you get the surprise! Rose

It didn't make sense. We finished the movie and fell asleep during the next one. After breakfast the next morning, I thought about the text and decided to wait until I got home to call Rose to see what the *surprise* was all about. We gathered our things together, as Paw and Maw Mack had made arrangements to drop us off at our homes. The car was loaded, and we all jumped in. Paw Mack pushed the remote to open the garage door, and as he backed out, the Mackster exclaimed, "Paw, you and Maw have been tee-peed."

"What?" exclaimed Paw Mack.

"You're kidding, right?" questioned Maw Mack as she turned to look.

As Maw Mack turned, she saw all five of us pointing to the trees, the bushes, and the lawn in the front of the house. Paw Mack put the car in park and said, "Well, boys, guess what we're doing?"

Some Things to Think About

1. What are your grandparents like?

2. Tell about a funny situation that happened with your grandparents or an elderly couple.

3. Has your house ever been toilet papered? If so, do you know who did it?

4. Have you ever worked around your house and gotten paid for it? If so, what did you do to earn the money?

5. What would you buy if you had some extra money to spend?

Understanding Girls ... or Not!

Boys are from logic while girls are from the twilight zone.

I got on the phone with Rose and tried to act like I was mad. I even tried to argue with her, but it was no use. It was then that I more fully realized what the sign meant that I read out at Tex's ranch when on our campout. I recall the sign read: There's Two Theories to Arguing with a Woman ... Neither One Works!

Yes, sir, I tell you that those girl folk just don't think the way us boy folk do. Whoever came up with the rhyme that goes like this: *Girls are made out of sugar and spice and everything nice, but boys are made out of slugs and snails and puppy dog tails ...* well, I can say there weren't any boys on the committee that made up *that* rhyme.

At school on Monday, I passed Rose in the halls three or four times. Each time, she saw me and then quickly turned away. *What did I do?* I thought to myself. After I got off the phone with her, I thought everything was all right. I asked Tex what the problem might be, but he said to ignore her for now. The next day, I tried that. The day after that one, I got a phone text that read: *Why are you ignoring me?*

What to do now? As the Nose and I were talking in the cafeteria at lunchtime, I asked him what I should do to get myself out of this situation. His advice was to tell her a funny joke. I took his advice willingly and sent her this text:

Knock, knock. Who's there? Boo. Boo who? What are you crying for?

I thought, as I hit the send button, that *that* would do the trick and get me out of this mess. Just a few minutes went by, and I learned that not only did it *not* work, but things were getting worse, as I received this text from Rose: *Silly ... don't you know that knock-knock jokes went out a long time ago?*

Now what?

"Is she playing games with me?" I asked the Mackster as we left school that afternoon. In desperation, I asked him for advice.

He responded by saying, "A poem. Write her a poem and make it real mushy too."

"Okay," I said. And so I did.

Roses are red, violets are blue, is there anyone nicer than you?

I thought that was pretty good, but I soon found out that it wasn't. Her text read: *Ugh! Old school! What closet did you get that out of!*

There is a saying that says: *If you find yourself in a hole, then the first thing you need to do is stop digging!*

Good advice, I suppose, but I was desperate, and desperation doesn't take too well to good reasoning. So off I went to get advice from Slo-Mo. His first suggestion was to ignore her.

"Done that," I said.

His next suggestion was to tell her a joke.

"Done that too," I responded.

"How about a poem," he recommended. "I heard that worked for Joe when he was having his troubles with Janet."

"Already tried that too," I said.

Slo-Mo just stood there, shook his head, and finally said, "I'm all out of ideas, so I guess you're on your own, ole pal. Good luck."

Next Saturday, we gathered at my house and raced on our bikes to the DQ. I didn't win. In fact, I came in dead last. I didn't even race through the door when the Mackster yelled, "Last one in is a rotten egg." Ms. Wanda was there and took our orders. After we gave her our orders, I slowly walked to the booth as the others were running to it. Ms. Wanda called me back, and I slowly turned around and approached her.

"Blake," she said. "What's with the sad face?"

"Sad face?" I responded as I put on a forced smile. "What are you talking about?"

"Don't give me that. I've heard the news," she said.

"What news?" I innocently inquired.

"Rose was in here earlier," she said.

"What?" I responded.

"Yes, she was," Ms. Wanda stated. "And her face was just about as sad looking as yours. You don't need to tell me anything. Enjoy your ice cream."

"I need your help," I blurted out.

"I see," Ms. Wanda knowingly said. After I told her what had happened, she presented to me a plan.

"A plan is like a recipe for making a cake," she explained. "If the step-by-step recipe instructions are not followed, then the desired result will be lost. You must follow the recipe, or plan, exactly for the result you want," she concluded.

"I will," I obediently said.

So, just as planned, I went to the DQ the following Saturday. Ms. Wanda had instructed me to text Rose just before I left my house to come to DQ, with these words: *I'm at DQ. Meet me ... now!*

"That's all and nothing more," Ms. Wanda commanded. "A girl likes a boy who, in a confident and mild way, takes charge," she said.

After I entered the DQ, I told Ms. Wanda that I had sent the text, and then she told me to take a seat in a booth by the window so I would be able to see when Rose approached.

"What if she doesn't come?" I said doubtfully.

"This is a test," Ms. Wanda coolly replied. "But I'd bet a great deal of money, if I were a betting person, that she'll be here."

I waited for a very long time, at least ten minutes. I then saw a pink speck in the distance. Soon it got bigger, and I noticed it was a pink bike with a girl on it with long, flowing, black hair. The bike and girl were going really fast. Ms. Wanda saw her too, and turning to me, she gave me a smile and a wink.

"Here she comes into the parking lot. I hope she slows down so she doesn't run into the building," Ms. Wanda said.

"If all my buds and I had been racing, and Rose were racing with us today," I said to Ms. Wanda, "Rose would seriously be the winner."

"No doubt," responded Ms. Wanda as Rose laid her bike down just outside the front door. Ms. Wanda then quickly slid back behind the customer counter.

Rose coolly opened the door, walked in, stopped, and looked around.

Wow! There she was in her hot pink capris, a white, almost sleeveless top, and the coolest sunglasses I'd ever seen. Oh, and a hot pink hat with her shiny, black ponytail poking out of the back and going a little more than midway down her back. Her hat had white lettering that read: Can't Touch This!

I was flabbergasted, and my head began to swirl. I refocused and then caught the lettering on her shirt that read: Don't Try to Understand Me. Just Love Me!

I was getting cold feet and wanted to back out of the whole plan thing. My mind told me that I couldn't go through with it. But then my eye caught hold of Ms. Wanda in the background. She looked at me and motioned with her head for me to implement the plan. I thought of the saying that goes: *When the going gets tough, the tough get going!*

All at once, that saying and Ms. Wanda's head nod started something inside me that motivated me to get going. Although we were already looking at each other, I raised my hand and motioned Rose over to me. Rose approached and stopped in front of me and started to speak. Before she could get her second word out, I raised my finger to her lips and said, "Shhhhhh." We sat down, and then right on cue, Ms. Wanda brought over one, not two, but *one* of the largest, double-scooped, chocolate-syrup-dripped, nuttiest sundaes that one could ever imagine … with two red spoons, one poking out on each side. A smile covered both of our faces as we dug in to eat.

Close to finishing and after good conversation, I reached for *the thing* that was next to me on my seat. Without saying a word, I picked it up and placed it in front of Rose. It was a small box, giftwrapped, with an oversized bow on top.

Rose could not and would not take her eyes off of the box. Finally, I pushed the box over to her and said, "A little something for you." A little more conversation, and then Rose excused herself to return home. I walked her to the door, and then she rode off on her bike.

"Well, Blake, it looks like you got an official girlfriend," said Ms. Wanda.

"Looks that way," I said. "But somehow I feel like the dog that chases the car, and then when the car stops, the dog doesn't know what to do with it."

Before I left, I asked Ms. Wanda, "What is it that girls like so much about getting a present?"

She responded by explaining, "Everybody likes to get presents because of the element of surprise. But girls especially like to get presents from someone they like because it tells them that the giver likes them too."

I thanked Ms. Wanda and left the DQ with a big smile of understanding and accomplishment.

Some Things to Think About

1. Do you have a girlfriend or boyfriend or a close friend? How did you meet her or him?

2. Do you like getting presents?

3. What is the best present you have ever received? Who gave you that present?

4. What is the best present you have ever given?

5. What do you think Blake gave to Rose?

The Dance

What to do? When in doubt ... shout!

"Weekends. It seems that lots of things happen on weekends," I said as I spoke in front of the bathroom mirror. Just at that time, Bengy passed by the open bathroom door. He continued a step more and then made a 180-degree turn and poked his head in the doorway.

"Not true, Blake," Bengy said.

Even without my invitation for him to continue, he did.

"It's been my observation, and I've even noticed, as I refresh my memory by looking through my notes," he said as he pretended to have a notepad that he was searching through, "that if people don't have things that happen to them over the weekend, then they invent things that they *do*, thus giving them something to talk about on Mondays to impress their friends and acquaintances, which most likely aren't their friends anyway. Why, you might wonder? Because if they were their friends, they wouldn't feel the need to impress them."

"Thank you, Mr. Know It All," I said. But he continued as if he hadn't heard my words or even noticed my presence.

"It has been my experience that ..." Bengy continued.

I got out of the bathroom as fast as I could and left Bengy to himself. Besides, I had to get to school early. So I rushed past the kitchen area and heard a voice that stopped me in my tracks.

"Where are you going so early this morning?" my mom spoke.

"I just need to get to school early today because I need to go to tutorials and get some help with science," I hurriedly responded.

"You get some breakfast down you first," Mom commanded.

I gulped down some orange juice and a piece of toast with grape jam on it. I then hustled myself out the side door, jumped on my bike, rode to school, strolled up to my regular hangout area, and waited. One by one, my buds arrived. Each time one approached, they asked about me and Rose. Each time, I asked, "How do you know about me and Rose?" And each time, they referred me to the Nose. About that time, the Nose walked over.

"Well, His Nose has arrived, but where is the rest of him?" inquired Tex.

"He'll be here ... eventually," said the Mackster.

"So, I guess you want to know how I found out what I know,"

said the Nose knowingly. He then pointed his forefinger to his nose, and while tapping it, he exclaimed, "The Nose knows, it knows all things, and all things are known by the nose. So what do you want to know that the nose can tell you? Go ahead and ask the Nose." He then did a two-handed patty-cake roll while bowing.

"Rose, we're talking about Rose and Blake. Explain to Blake about how you came to know about him and Rose," encouraged Slo-Mo.

"Yes, please," said the others.

"Yeah, Nose, how come you know so much yet so little?" I said.

"The Nose knows all—"

"Okay," I interrupted. "We know all of that, but what about Rose and me."

"What about Rose and you? Am I a fortune teller," the Nose playfully commented.

"No, but you know … and your nose … and all that stuff. Come on, Nose, *give it up!*" I demanded with finality.

"All righty then, I'll tell you," he retorted. "Rose told Jessie. Jessie told her best friend, Alexa. Alexa then told her best friend, Freda. Freda then told Catherina. Catherina didn't say anything to any of her friends, but she did tell her mother. Her mother bowls with Ms. Wanda on a bowling league on Sunday evenings."

"Okay, but that doesn't explain how *you* found out," I said.

"Oh, yeah," the Nose recalled. "My mom bowls on the same team."

"Wow," Tex said to the Nose. "Talking to you is like the dog that chases its tail around in a circle with hopes of catching it. The only thing it gets you is a dizzy headache."

"Hey, here comes Rose," the Mackster observed. "Guess you gotta be going, huh?"

Rose walked up close and stopped.

"Sure do. See you boys later," I said as I walked toward Rose.

I stopped just in front of Rose, and then she turned and stepped beside me. She looked down at my hand, and I got a felling I was supposed to do something, so I did. I gently clasped her hand with mine. She smiled, and we walked into the school. Once inside and a little past the doors, Rose came to a sudden stop. Hanging on a wall just outside the attendance office was a gigantic sign that read:

Sixth-Grade Dance and Games this Saturday
In the Auditorium
7–9 p.m.

I vaguely remember the announcements, and I am sure the signs were not put up over the weekend, but I can't recall seeing them hanging up on the walls any time the week before either … but surely they must have been there. I suddenly got that same *I need to do something* feeling that prompted me to hold Rose's hand earlier. *What* was I supposed to do? *That* was the question.

Then, suddenly and without thought, I realized we better get going to class or we might be tardy. So I said, "We should go."

Rose responded with a cheerful, "Yes, I'd love to!" Off she scampered with Jezzie, who was passing by, to their class. As they walked away, I could hear Jezzie and Rose talking about the dance.

I turned down the hallway and thought, *What am I going to do? I don't even know how to dance!*

Some Things to Think About

1. Can you relate to Blake and his situation?

2. Can you relate to Rose and her thinking?

3. Do you know how to dance?

4. What advice could you give to Blake?

5. Would you react to Blake the way his buds did? How would your reaction be similar?

   How would your reaction be different?

6. Describe a boy or a girl you would want to take to a dance.

Mistake or Mistaken

Give me some of that ole rock and roll.
That's the kind of music that soothes my soul!

Bengy has always been known for being a good dancer; I do have to admit that. So, swallowing my pride, I went to him for help.

"This ain't gonna be your mamma's hokey pokey," Bengy said as he lined us up in two lines.

Yes, I talked my buds into going to the dance too. I wasn't going to go down or be made a fool of *alone*. So there we were standing in front of the great dance teacher, Bengy the Magnificent. Well, that's what he demanded we call him if he was going to give lessons for free … so we did. We weren't giving up our ice-cream money for this, that's for sure!

"Rule number one," said Bengy the Magnificent. "Any time you put your hand out in front of you and shake it, never say, 'And do the hokey pokey and turn yourself about.' Got it?"

"Got it," we agreed.

"Rule number two." Bengy the Magnificent continued. "Never say, 'Simon says,' when you move your head back and forth. That goes for sideways too. Got it?"

"Yes, sir, Oh Great One," said the Mackster.

"You're *supposed* to say the Magnificent, but I'll accept Oh Great One too," Bengy responded. "Now get those lines straight," he barked. "Anyway, what kind of a dance studio do you think I'm running here?"

As we straightened up our lines, Slo-Mo asked, "Mr. Magnificent, you mean there's more to dancing than what we've already learned so far?"

"Yeah, you mean there's more?" inquired the Mackster.

"You weenies are just getting started," he said.

"But I got homework to do," stated the Nose.

Bengy butted in with, "What do I have to work with here? Sounds like a bunch of belly-aching, butt-scratching, no-good, lost-in-the-world, sniffling-nosed crybabies, bed wettin'—"

"Okay, that's getting a little personal now," stammered Slo-Mo.

We all looked at Slo-Mo, and then I piped up and said, "Okay, let's get on with this."

Bengy continued, "Now when you put your left leg out, remember *not* to say, 'And do the hokey pokey.' That goes for your right leg too. Got it?"

"Yes, Oh Great One," we sang together.

For fifteen more minutes, we practiced the moves and not saying, "Simon says" or the "hokey pokey" thing, although we did have to remind Slo-Mo, as on one occasion he mistakenly said, "Simon says."

"Is that all, Oh Great One?" I asked.

"One last thing," Bengy said. "If you ever get stuck not knowing what to do, or if you run out of things to do ..."

"Yes?" we said.

Bengy continued, "Give out a big yell! Now get out of here."

Whooping and hollering, we left.

My buds and I arrived at the dance fashionably but only slightly late, as my mom dropped us off.

"I'll be back at nine," she said as she drove off.

As we entered the auditorium, the dance floor was packed with dancers, and a cool song was playing.

"I think Bengy must have taught all of these people to dance," the Nose said.

"I think you're right," answered the Mackster.

"Ain't nothing like I've ever seen," stated Tex.

"Let's do this," I said, "before I lose my confidence and chicken out."

The ratio of girls to boys was about two to one, so my buds didn't have much trouble finding a dance partner. Soon I located Rose, and after a little self-encouraging, I asked her to dance. To my surprise and without any explanation, she said, "No." I was taken back but at the same time a little relieved. But then I saw my buds out on the dance floor bobbing and kicking and testing out their lessons ... and they looked pretty good.

Rose and I sat on some chairs at the side of the dance floor ... watching. Conversation was a bit stiff but picked up as the dance number stopped and the others joined us. And then it was back out on the floor for all, except for Rose and me. She once again said no to my request to dance. Between the dance numbers,

Rose was the life of the group, but while the others were dancing, she was not.

The music stopped, and the announcer said it was time to play a game. Five students were selected to be "it." These "its" would run around and touch others. "As you are touched," the announcer said, "you must sit down." The last one would then be recognized, and the dancing would continue. This lasted for about five minutes, with all the screaming that my ears could take ... but it was fun. Rose thoroughly enjoyed herself and was almost the last one touched. The next song began as I sat next to Rose.

Rose scooted closer to me and, leaning over, said, "I really am having a good time with you, but ..."

"But what?" I coolly said.

"I've never danced before at a dance like this, and ... I don't know how," she shyly stated.

An idea rushed through my head. I caught hold of Rose's hand and said, "Follow me, little lady."

"Not to the dance floor," she said in protest.

"No, not to the dance floor," I assured her.

I led Rose out of the auditorium, slightly down a hallway and out of student traffic. About five minutes later, we reemerged to the auditorium. I held Rose's hand and asked, "Are you ready?" She reluctantly said yes. Just as we stepped onto the dance floor, the song was over, and the dancing stopped. The next song soon began, and I led Rose out once again to the dance floor. As we kicked, threw out our arms, and tossed our heads, we reminded each other not to say, "Simon says" or "do the hokey pokey."

While we were dancing, Tex and his partner danced their way over close to us. Tex's partner leaned over and whispered in Rose's ear. I later asked what she said. Rose stated that she said "how natural we look together and what great dancers we are." We laughed and had the best of times the rest of the evening. Every once in a while, Rose and I would hear one of my buds let out a shout. We gave a yell a time or two also.

My dad dropped everyone off at their homes, and as I walked into my house, Mom was sitting in a chair reading a book. The book was called *Rocking Chair Confessions.*

To make conversation, I asked, "Liking your book?"

Putting down the book, she responded, "Oh, hi, Blake honey. Yes, it's about secrets. Do you have any to tell me about the dance tonight? I'm all ears." She was grinning.

Some Things to Think About

1. Were you surprised that neither Blake nor Rose knew how to dance?

2. How did you learn to dance?

3. Have you ever tried to teach someone else something? What was it and how did you do it?

4. If you have a boyfriend or girlfriend, how do your friends react to them?

5. What is the name of your favorite song?

6. What kind of music do you listen to?

7. Do you know all of the words to a song? Write out that song.

What's Happening?

*Research experiments are like hamburger wrappers:
use them today, throw them away tomorrow,
and then recycle them the day after that.*

The dance was great, and the talk with my mom after the dance was good too. Rose looked prettier than ever, and even my brother, Bengy, seemed *almost* normal. Further, I was back on my game as I won the next Saturday's bike race to DQ. I completed my traditional victory dance around my bike, accompanied with my finger-pointing, hand-waving, number-one shout. Yes, I was on top of the world, and I planned to do everything I could to stay there.

I felt like subject number two of the experimenters that wanted to observe the various reactions of subjects to a certain situation. So these experimenters decided to put a dump truck of horse manure in the middle of a round barn. The experimenters sent subject number one into the barn and then closed the door for what was to be two minutes. Through a one-way glass window, they were to observe the behavior of the subject. They observed that subject number one began to cry, and the crying became more intense, so the experimenters took the young child out early at the parents' request.

A little later, the experimenters brought a second child of the same age into the barn. After closing the door, this child gazed at the pile of manure, slowly walked around it, and then jumped right in the middle of the big pile of manure while digging frantically. Surprised, the experimenters began scribbling notes, as this kind of behavior had not been observed before.

To complete their research, the experimenters afterward interviewed the two subjects. They brought in subject number one and asked him, "What were you thinking after you entered the barn and the door was closed?" The child responded that he didn't like the smell, and there was nothing to do, so he just sat down and began to cry. "Thank you for your answers," the experimenters said and then dismissed the subject back to his parents.

The experimenters then brought in subject number two and asked him the same question. Subject number two responded, "I looked around the room with this big pile of horse manure. I knew that there was no way out since the doors were all closed. It was then that I decided to jump right into the pile and start digging to locate the pony that had to be there somewhere. And I'm sure I would have found it if you guys had given me more time."

Not too long ago, my dad told me that story, and it has helped me to be more positive and look for the best in things even though the situation might not be very positive. Stories like that one are easy to remember and talk about. I began to get a funny feeling, the kind I get just before a test. I was new to this *love* business, and although I really did like Rose, girls are just different and not so easy to discuss things with.

I can talk to my buds about all kinds of things. We can talk all day long about bikes and bike racing, also about how good it feels to sleep out under the night sky. And we can ponder universal questions like how many minutes does it take a snail to travel from one crack in the sidewalk to the next crack in the sidewalk? One time, the Nose, the Mackster, Slo-Mo, Tex, and I conversed for over an hour about the various ways to hold a shooter marble when playing marbles.

But when I was with Rose, it was different, and I felt different from when I was with my buds. It didn't start out that way though. One time we were walking and talking—well actually, Rose was talking, and I was listening. She likes me to be a good listener and says I'm good at it. Well, like I said, Rose was talking, and I hadn't said much, so I began talking about my jars of marbles.

I told Rose that I had a whole bunch of marbles and that I had many different colored ones too. Some of the marbles were green, blue, red, black, yellow, white, and some had two colors. I even had a clear one, which were very hard to find. I was about to continue when she abruptly stopped walking. Suddenly, she quickly opened up her purse. Then she fumbled around and pulled out a small, round object.

As she twisted the top of the round object, it became a mirror, which she held very close to her face. She didn't say

"Stop talking" or anything like that. Her eyes started to droop, and then she said without explanation, "I have to go." And like a bullet, off she went.

At lunch, I huddled around my buds and told them what had happened.

"You shouldn't have talked about marbles," said the Mackster as he swallowed a bite of spaghetti.

"Yeah, really," said the Nose as he sucked soda through his straw.

"Okay, Tex, what do you say?" I inquired.

"Looks like you got girl troubles," Tex returned.

"Don't look at me. I got enough troubles of my own," retorted Slo-Mo.

"You sure do," we all said as we laughed.

The rest of the day went slowly, and Rose didn't meet me after school. I finally made it home and threw my backpack on the bed, which bounced twice and then off and onto the floor. Two seconds later, I followed and crashed onto the bed and fell into a light sleep. I heard Bengy trying to sing in his room across the hall.

I raised my head about three inches and said, "Keep it quiet in there," and then I dropped my head back down. It was peaceful for about fifteen seconds, and then Bengy appeared at my door.

"Blake?" said Bengy. "Is that you almost sleeping at four o'clock in the afternoon?"

"Yeah, *almost*," I said. "Except someone is howling, sick, or almost dying in the next room. I hear awful noises coming through the walls."

As I lay there face-down, I thought about how Bengy had taught me and my buds how to dance and had gotten us out of that jam for the sixth-grade dance a few weeks earlier. In one of my weaker moments, I actually began thinking that Bengy was a fairly decent older brother and maybe, just maybe … I quickly rolled over and raised my head and said, "Bengy."

Bengy was not there, but then I heard a faint response that said, "What."

Bengy then appeared back at my door, and I quickly said, "I need help. It's about Rose. I don't understand her."

Some Things to Think About

1. Are you sometimes confident, feeling like you're on top of the world?

2. What makes you feel good?

3. Do you get down in the dumps occasionally?

4. What helps you get out of the dumps?

5. Do you have a friend, a parent, grandparent, or older brother or sister who helps you in difficult times?

6. What special things do special people do to help you in a difficult time?

7. What do you do to help someone that needs your help?

Let's Shake Things Up

Friends...who needs one? I do!

"Calm down, Blake," Bengy said with a snort. "A girl, or a Rose, by any other name is still a girl or a Rose. I heard or read that somewhere. Anyway, what's got you down?"

"Rose and I were walking and talking," I explained, "and then all of a sudden she just up and walked away and avoided me the rest of the day. I don't get it!"

Bengy didn't say a word. He kept rubbing his chin, and finally I said, "This is not the time for itching or scratching. *Do* or *say something* ... and *stop* rolling your eyes!"

"Sorry, Blake, it's the way I get inspiration. But you're not telling me everything, now are you?"

"I'm not following you. I don't get it. What do you mean?" I said.

"I want the rest of the story ... all of it," Bengy demanded.

I started all over again, but then Bengy immediately held up his hand for me to stop. I waited as he left the room and returned shortly with his Sherlock Holmes cap on.

"Now I'm ready. Continue," he stated confidently.

Shaking my head, I continued. "As I was saying, Rose and I were walking and talking—"

"Stop," Bengy said. "Where were you?"

"Ooooh, brother. We were at school, Bengy. We were at school!" I said.

"Where at school?" Bengy inquired. "Were you in the cafeteria, in class, or in one of the halls?"

"In the hallway, and we had just passed one of the water fountains ... on the right, no, on the left side," I stated.

"Okay, the picture is becoming clearer," Bengy calmly said. "Whose left was the water fountain on, yours or Rose's?"

"It doesn't matter. *Both* of our left side. How's that?"

"So, you were not facing each other. Okay, that works for me," stated Bengy. "I just wanted to make sure both of you were walking in the same direction. Continue."

"Oh, so there we were—"

"Who's we? Please explain *we*," Bengy demanded.

"Oh, good grief! Heavens to Mercatroid and all of that! We," I continued, "were changing classes from second period going to third period. Like I said, Rose and I were walking and talking—"

"What were you talking about," Bengy asked as he leaned back and peered at me.

"Well, Rose was doing *all* of the talking, so I decided to *say* something, so I brought up my marble collection. You know, the marbles I keep on my closet shelf."

"Yes, I'm aware of them," Bengy stated as he rolled his eyes. "They're the same ones I heard last weekend going bang and clang all night when your friends were over, right?"

"Yeah, they would be the ones," I said.

"Ummmm," Bengy mused as he softly positioned his cupped hand under his jaw. "This is getting interesting. So what else happened?"

"That's about it," I stated. "Wait," I said. "This may or may not have any bearing on the situation, but she did reach down in her purse and got out a mirror."

"Go on," Bengy encouraged. "Something is still missing."

"Uh, well, she did have her hand close to her face just before reaching into her purse," I proudly recalled.

"Maybe there's something to that. I'll get back to you and let you know," Bengy said as he left the room.

Not knowing how long it would take Bengy to respond, I called the Nose to put his network in place to find out what was going on. I figured if I had two people working various angles, at least one of them might pull through with some information I could use. I just finished texting the Nose when Bengy rushed in and declared he had some news. I was ready to listen to anything.

"I've got it, Blake," Bengy stated enthusiastically. "Rose had developed a zit and discovered it when walking with you. She didn't want you to see her with a zit, so she ditched you to save herself the embarrassment. *Walla,* there you have it and thank you very much," he proudly exclaimed.

"That's the stupidest explanation I've ever heard," I said as I walked out.

Shortly after I left Bengy to himself, I got a text from the Nose that read: *Feelers are out ... should know something soon.*

A little later in the evening, I got a one-word text from Rose that read: *Sorry.*

What was going on? Sorry? How was I supposed to take that or even understand what it meant? Sorry that I don't want to see you anymore? Sorry that you're just not my type? Sorry that you're a sorry guy? Sorry, but you're not the best I can do? Or you're just plain old sorry! Ouch, that last one would really hurt. I couldn't and didn't want to think anymore.

"Tomorrow is another day," I said, and then I went to sleep with my school clothes still on.

Some Things to Think About

1. How is Blake feeling?

2. Have you had a bad day like Blake is having?

3. How do you get out of the dumps? Does someone help you get out of the dumps or do you get out by yourself?

4. When have you helped someone in a situation like Blake's? Were they thankful? How did you feel after it was all over?

I'm Sorry? No, I'm Happy!

Take that! Take that! And take that!
I hope you feel miserable now!

I slept through the night. I must have been exhausted. The next morning, I woke up, slid over to my cell phone, and checked my messages. The Nose was trying to get a hold of me with some important news. He had texted me several times, but I had been out like a light. His last text read: *You're not responding—see you at school in the morning with news.*

I hurriedly got dressed but found I had some extra time, so I stood in front of the mirror and stared. I grabbed a comb and brush and began doodling with my hair. I tried various styles, but none appealed to me.

After a while, I remembered a hairstyle I saw in a magazine, called a fohawk. I rushed to my room and opened a magazine but couldn't find a picture of the fohawk on any of the pages. I reached for another magazine and went through it but still couldn't find the picture. I grabbed another magazine, and finally on page 34, it was there.

It looked cooler than I had remembered. I raced back to the bathroom and laid the magazine on the counter next to me. I spread open the page and pressed it as flat as I could get it. Using the picture as my guide, I began to brush. The more I brushed, the cooler I looked. I even threw my collar up. I then turned sideways; first I turned to my right and then to my left. Peering straight forward, I nodded my head in an approving manner. The guy in the mirror looked back at me and gave me two big thumbs-up, and then he walked away with a gigantic smile.

I arrived at school and saw my buds as I approached our gathering place. They were in a semicircle, and Slo-Mo noticed me first. He glanced at me and quickly turned to the others and said, "Who's the new guy?" At that point, they all turned to look. Laughter filled the air from four of the dumbest-looking guys on campus. I even told them how *dumb* they looked.

"What's your name?" asked the Mackster.

"None of your bee's wax," I said.

"Well, *none of your bee's wax*, glad to meet you," remarked the Nose.

"Who's your hair stylist?" asked Tex.

Laughter filled the air once again. About that time, Nancy and Jezzie walked by and said, "Like your hair, Blake!"

Jezzie then added, "It looks cool. I wish your pals would do something with their hair. I think Rose will like it too."

"Thanks, Jezzie. Thanks, Nancy," I responded as they continued on.

"Now what do you think about me, huh?" I said as I imitated a moon walk. "Chacow, take that, and that, and that. Booya! You haven't a clue, do ya," I continued as I strutted around the boys.

I was caught up in my performance and then remembered my Rose dilemma. I abruptly stopped, turned, and walked over to the Nose.

"What do you have for me, Nose?"

"You wish to speak to the all-knowing Nose, do you?"

"Yes, I do. Have you seen him?" I asked.

"Yeah, I'm right in front of you, Blake. Can't you see me?"

"Well, I see a big nose in front of me, but I'm wondering where *you* are," I said with a snicker.

"Okay, Blake, do you want to know what I know or not?" the Nose said.

"Lay it on me. I can take it. Give it to me straight now, and don't sugarcoat it," I said.

Grinning, the Nose burst out, "Your hair—it's getting to me. I'm having a hard time concentrating when I look at you."

"All right then, don't look at me, but give it to me straight," I responded.

The Nose cleared his face and began. "I put my feelers out just like I told you I would, and here's what I got. My traditional feelers only told me that Rose went to the restroom and applied some makeup after she left you. Cindy told me that, as she was in the restroom at the same time. Cindy and Rose also have third period together. Other avenues I checked with came up empty, so I went to my last and usually best source ... Talking Shirley."

The Nose continued by saying, "Talking Shirley is my contact on Facebook. She won't let just anybody have access."

"How did you come to be Facebook friends with her?" I interrupted.

"Well, it's like this. I'm good at math, and she's not, so I help her with her math. I've been helping her all year long, and access to her social network has proven very beneficial. All the neat school gossip is there and better than any others I visited or heard about. That leads me to my next bit of information, you and Rose."

"Please continue," I requested.

As the Nose continued, ours ears leaned in to hear more clearly. "Rose was seen exiting the restroom after applying makeup to her face. According to Cindy, Rose spent extra time on one specific area of her face, the left upper cheek. Talking Shirley scoured her pages on the Rose incident and found that Rose confided in Beverly that she didn't want anyone to see her in that condition.

"Talking Shirley then searched and found that Marlene posted that 'the condition was a zit that had suddenly popped up on Rose's left cheek and that even after makeup, it wasn't enough to satisfy Rose and her concerns.' That's not all. Martha posted that 'concern for Blake not to see Rose is important.' When I found that out, I called Martha. She further related that she sent out texts to all her friends around the school to help Rose avoid seeing you and you seeing her. There you have it all in a nutshell, and it didn't cost you a dime."

"Wow, so it was a zit after all," I said. In the back of my mind, I recalled Bengy's original conclusion and how I had reacted. Suddenly, out of my side vision, I got a glimpse of Rose standing a few feet away. I looked long and hard at her. I could vaguely see the place where the zit was to have been, but I couldn't detect it. Well, maybe just a tad bit red, but other than that, Rose was nothing but beauty.

Regaining myself, I briskly walked over to Rose's side. She was simply beautiful. She looked down at my hand, and I got that familiar feeling I was supposed to do something. I reached down and took hold of her hand. She smiled approvingly. She kept looking at me and then finally broke the silence.

"I really like your hair," she said.

"I really like your hair too," I returned.

"Now, tell me more about your marble collection ..."

The rest of the day went just great, as things were back to normal. But the following day had a surprise waiting for me. As I walked up to our regular meeting place at school, I got the surprise of my life. Instead of my buds, there were four new dudes standing where we normally got together. I was a little hesitant to approach at first, but upon closer examination, I noticed the dudes all had fohawk haircuts. I walked on up to these new dudes and entered their circle.

I said, "I'm Blake. Are you dudes new to this school?" We burst out in laughter and had a hard time stopping. That was the ending of our sixth grade year, and what a year it was! So seventh grade, look out 'cause here we come!

Some Things to Think About

1. Has something like this happened to you?

2. Have you ever changed something about you? If so, what was it that you changed? How did others react to you, and what did they say? Was the reaction positive? Did you keep the change or go back to the same as before?

3. Have you ever made a change that others followed, doing the same as you had?

Humpty Dumpty sat on a wall.
Humpty Dumpty had a great fall.
His classmates tried to put him back together ... yes, did they all,
But only Humpty could do it ... that was his call.

About the Author

Delbert Doyce Pape was born to Raymond and Verba (Jones) Pape in Hillsboro, Texas, in 1951 (fourth of seven children). In the third grade, his family moved from Portales, New Mexico, to San Angelo, Texas, and he graduated from San Angelo Central High School in 1970. Del worked at a local hamburger drive-through restaurant in San Angelo called the Charcoal House; this lasted from his freshman year of high school until his first year of college at Angelo State University. While attending ASU, he met and married Linda Lee (Ward) Benson (first of seven children) of Barksdale, Texas, whose parents are Ira (stepfather) and Ruth Ward.

In 1971, Del joined the United States Air Force and trained and worked as a radar technician. After ten months of training in Biloxi, Mississippi, Del and Linda took their family for an assignment to Kalispell (radar site), Montana, for three years. Afterward, Del was assigned to a twelve-month remote tour in Alaska and then a four-year assignment at Duluth International Airport in Duluth, Minnesota. At this point, Del completed a degree in Psychology from Chapman University and was accepted into an Officer Training School program, which led to his being commissioned a second lieutenant officer. Afterward, the family saw an assignment to Beale Air Force Base, California, for four years. Del and Linda were now accompanied with five children: Peter, Lisa, Andy, Jace, and Ben.

From California, they were sent to Plattsburgh, New York, and stayed for two years. Afterward, they saw a trip to Offutt

Air Force Base, Nebraska, for four years. While at Offutt, Del completed a master's degree in Public Administration through the University of Oklahoma's "Classroom without Walls" program. Next came four years at Dyess Air Force Base in Abilene, Texas, and retirement occurred in December of 1994. While assigned to Dyess AFB, Del spent four months at Riyadh Air Base, Saudi Arabia, in support of "Desert Shield/Storm."

After retirement, Del became a Child Protective Services case manager for the State of Texas and served in Baird, Texas, in that capacity for two years. Later, he became a certified special education teacher at Wylie Independent School District in Abilene, Texas, from 1997 until 2009. In 2009, Del taught at Goose Creek Consolidated ISD in Baytown, Texas, as a social studies teacher from 2009 until his retirement in June of 2012.

Finally, he authored his first published book (September 2012) titled, *Rocking Chair Confessions: Tales Told by a Texan ... Some Partially True!*